GARDEN OF DISCOVERY & LOVE

VAMPIRES OF NEW ORLEANS
BOOK 3

Madalyn Rae

For my readers. This isn't the finale of Amelia's story, but her life is going to look a little different from here on out.

Thank you for reading and sharing my love of story telling!

the trip from hell

THE MOMENT the private jet ascends into the sky, my stomach leaps into my throat. Viktor's been the epitome of a broody vampire, and I'm on the edge of a very human action—throwing up. This has all the makings for a trip of a lifetime.

"Can I get you something to drink?" the dark-haired attendant asks on her latest trip down the aisle. No doubt, my face matches the turmoil in my soul.

"No, I don't think that will help. Thank you for the offer."

"First time flying?" She leans her hip against the seat in front of me.

I look toward Viktor. "In a plane...yes. This is the first time I've flown." She doesn't look confused by my almost admission of flying with a vampire.

"May I sit with you?" Her accent is a mixture of *Highlander* and *Monty Python.*

"Of course. I could use the distraction." I take a deep breath, hoping to suppress the nausea in the base of my throat. "I love your accent. Where are you from?"

"Thank you." She smiles warmly. "I'm from the Isle of Man, in the UK."

"Oh, wow! I did research on that island for my Ph.D. Did you know there are rumors of elementals living on the island?"

"Elementals? Like the little gremlins that relate with an earthly element?" She laughs awkwardly. "You don't say."

"Yeah, well, there are a lot of rumors and stories based on European culture. When I studied the Isle, it was one of only a few that mentioned elementals. It was mind-blowingly interesting. I wish I could've found more information."

"Where are you from?" She changes the subject quickly.

"Me? I'm from New Orleans. The Big Easy. The Crescent City. N'awlins." God, I sound like an idiot. Becoming a vampire didn't take away my awkwardness.

"My name is Sophie," she says, holding her hand toward me with a smile.

"Amelia." I shake her hand. "Thank you for the distraction. It's helping."

"Aye, of course." She turns toward Viktor. "Is he always so...grumpy?"

I turn toward the ancient vampire. "Yes. Completely. He can be an ass with a capital A."

"I can hear you," Viktor mumbles from across the plane. Since Celeste disappeared, whatever I thought was happening between us has come to a screeching halt. We enjoyed one night together and since then, nothing. It's like we're nothing more than roommates. With his immortal daughter missing, now is not the time for that conversation.

Sophie giggles. "He reminds me of my brother. He can be rather grumpy, too."

"Please tell me about him. Keep the distractions coming."

She sighs. "Well, he's freakishly tall and has bright red hair." She pulls away slightly. "It's nearly the same color as your roots. Tell me you didn't cover beautiful red hair?"

"I did once. It's a long story."

"In fact, you two could be related. He has your same eyes and coloring." She pulls her phone out of her pocket. "I'm going to text him and tell him I found his twin."

"Does he live on the same island as you?"

"Sometimes. He moves around a lot. Right now, he and his fiancé are in Iceland, but they go back and forth."

"Iceland? That's somewhere I'd love to visit. What's it like?"

"It's one of the most beautiful places on earth, also, one of the coldest. You definitely need to go!"

"Ladies and gentlemen, we are approaching Toussaint Louverture International Airport. Please secure any loose items and prepare to land," our nameless pilot announces.

"That's my cue." Sophie jumps up. "It was a pleasure to talk with you, Amelia. Maybe we'll meet again one day."

"I hope so. Thank you for your help." I follow her with my eyes as she moves across the aisle, pulling the newspaper out of Viktor's hands and instructing him to buckle his seat belt and wipe the grumpy look off of his face. To my surprise, he does it. Most humans sense there's something different about Viktor and either steer clear of him or try to molest him on the spot. Sophie doesn't seem fazed.

This airport in Haiti is different from the one in New Orleans. We exit, finding the tarmac full of people, wandering amongst the planes. "Why are people walking around on the tarmacs?"

"I wouldn't know," Viktor answers simply. It seems the grumpy version of him has returned. We push through the crowds and away from the airport.

"Where are we going?" I follow as close behind him as possible, barely able to keep up with the crowds. He keeps walking. "Viktor?" We continue pushing until it begins to thin out, allowing for easier movement. For as much as I can tell, I might as well be invisible.

Viktor leads us to an older model convertible parked on the side of the road. "Get in," he demands, opening the passenger door. I resist the urge to throw a tantrum and refuse. Instead, I swallow my pride and follow directions, climbing inside. He magically produces a key and pulls us away from the curb, driving until we're surrounded by nothing but farmland.

Thirty silent minutes later, we pull in front of a modest two-story stucco house. He enters a code, opens the front door, and ushers me inside quickly.

The inside looks nothing like I expected. The home is completely remodeled with modern features. Floor-to-ceiling glass walls surround what looks like a court-yard filled to the brim with exotic plants, swimming pools, and heavenly bliss. "This is beautiful. What is this place?"

"Your room is through there." Viktor moves to a room on the opposite side of the house without acknowledging my question.

"What the hell is your problem?" I follow him.

"I don't know what you're talking about."

I cross my arms across my chest. "Seriously? You don't know what I'm talking about?" I mimic his tone. He opens his suitcase and begins unpacking. "Viktor?" I step between the suitcase and him.

He stops, looking me in the eyes. "Amelia?" He turns in the other direction.

"Have I done something to upset you? You've been a complete asshole since we left New Orleans, and now we have separate rooms?" God, why am I asking if *I've* done something wrong? Carrying your trauma around much, Amelia?

He sighs deeply. "I thought you might appreciate some time to yourself."

"Time to myself? Is that what you think I want?"

"I don't know what you want," he raises his voice.

"I thought..."

"You thought what? That we were coming to Haiti to make love in the sand? Until my daughter is found, my happiness or anyone else's is of no importance."

Staring at the man, who less than seventy-two hours ago made love to me in every position available, I turn to leave, not sure what else to say. I completely understand that Celeste is the main character at this moment, but dammit, why does it have to hurt so much? Maybe I'm being selfish. My insecurity raises its little head once more.

"Amelia, wait," his tone is softer. "I'm sorry." I turn, facing him as he sits on the edge of the bed. "I don't...I don't know who I am without her," his voice is no louder than a whisper. "She's the reason I've lived. She's the reason I became a vampire. The reason I've... remained. I don't know who I am without her."

I sit next to him, not sure what to say. "Celeste is the smartest, most capable being I've ever met. You have done a remarkable job raising her. I don't claim to know what she's thinking, but I can say without a doubt, this is the last thing she would want for you. You have to be strong, for her. You can't give up." I wrap my fingers around his. "We're going to find her."

Viktor turns toward me. "Thank you, Amelia." I reach up, wiping a tear from his cheek.

"Don't push me away. Let me help you. I'm not an ancient vampire with unwavering strength, but I have knowledge of the world around us. I miss her and want her back, too."

He leans his head toward me, propping it on mine. "Thank you."

"You already said that." I kiss his cheek gently before standing and clapping my hands. "Now, where do we start?"

A loud knock on the door startles me. "Our guests have arrived." Stoic Viktor returns, as he moves to get up.

I stop his movement. "If we're going to do this, I need you to tell me everything. Don't keep secrets from me."

Viktor opens the door to a middle-aged woman and a young man who looks to be in his midtwenties. "Mr. Luquire?" the dark-skinned woman asks.

"Ms. Rose?"

"Yes, sir. This is my...assistant, Emmanuel."

Viktor opens the door wide. "Please, come in."

"This is beautiful," Rose says, looking around the home. Her strong accent makes it difficult to understand her words. "It's been a while since I've been on this side of the island."

The young man follows Rose into the living area. "Can I get you something to drink?" I ask, pretending I know where things are in this house.

"No, thank you." The two of them sit on the over-stuffed couch. "Let's not beat around the bush, Mr. Luquire. I was told you wanted to meet with me and my assistant, although without any context, I'm not sure why we are here."

"I would have thought the five million dollars that accompanied the request would've been context enough."

Rose sighs, reaching for the hand of Emmanuel. "I was promised that no harm would come to me or my assistant."

Viktor sighs. "I'm looking for someone." Rose nods, encouraging him to continue. "Someone who would have come looking for specific knowledge that only someone with a special set of skills would be privy to."

"Mr. Luquire, I'm not one to try to read between the lines. I can assure you that speaking freely is something you can do in your current company. That is if your friend here knows the truth." She nods her head toward me.

Viktor sighs. "You may speak freely."

"You two are both vampires." Her words are a statement, not a question. I stare blankly at the woman on the couch. She doesn't look the least bit nervous after her admission. "In fact, you, Mr. Luquire, are a very ancient vampire while your friend is quite the opposite. The one you seek with the knowledge isn't me, but I know who can help you." She turns toward the young man beside her. "Emmanuel needed the knowledge as well."

I turn my full attention to the younger man in front of me. "You were an immortal child?"

"I was." He smiles, showing a mouth full of white teeth.

"How?" Viktor asks.

"I believe that's the knowledge you're here to seek," Ms. Rose says with a smile.

"I think my daughter may have been here seeking the same information."

"I don't know anything about a child, but I can send you to a practitioner who might be able to help." She turns toward the young man. "My son was turned at a very young age. He was eight." She pats Emmanuel on the back. "That happened over three hundred years ago."

"Ms. Rose? Are you a vampire?" I ask.

"No," she answers with a smirk. "You want to know how I'm still alive?" I nod, and she clears her throat. "The magic that keeps me alive is similar to the magic that will help your daughter age."

"Emmanuel?" He turns toward my voice. "Are you healthy?"

"Yes, ma'am. I am."

"Where can we find this person with the knowl-edge?" Viktor asks.

"I will relay your questions and concerns to him, and he will be in contact." Rose and her son stand, ready to leave.

"That's not acceptable." Viktor moves closer to the duo.

"I'm afraid it will have to be, Mr. Luquire. I'm not afraid of you. You can't harm me."

"I wouldn't mean to do you harm. I apologize if that was implied." Viktor steps back, clearing his throat.

"He'll be in touch," she says, moving toward the door. "Thank you for your hospitality." The two of them exit the heavy wooden door and disappear from our lives.

"What the hell was that?"

Viktor runs a hand through his hair. "That was the answer to our dilemma."

"Dilemma? Is that what we're calling Celeste now?" Why am I getting angry? "Now what?"

"Now, we wait."

......

Three weeks have passed since we arrived on this island and still no contact. Viktor has become broody and withdrawn again, leaving me to my own devices and entertainment. This morning, I made my way to an outdoor market not too far from the house. The people of Haiti respond to me differently than at home. When I walk around New Orleans, humans sense me and make a wide berth to avoid contact. Here, no one pays me any attention. It's the most human I've felt in the nearly two years since being changed. I'm one of the crowd, and the anonymity is nice.

"That would look beautiful on you," a young woman says, watching me pick up a brightly colored linen wrap she has for sale on her table.

"It's beautiful. Did you make this?"

"I did." She smiles. "I will sell you two for the price of one." She digs through the pile of wraps, handing me a deep green version of the one in my hands. "This color suits you."

"I'll take them. Thank you." I pull out my unexchanged American money. "I'm sorry, all I have are American dollars."

"No worries. Five dollars American will cover the costs." I hand her a ten-dollar bill. Her eyes enlarge. "Oh, no. That's too much."

"No, it's not. Your work is worth ten times that."

"Thank you, ma'am."

I move through the market, purchasing a beautiful coral necklace, along with a brightly colored hair wrap, and I'm ready to purchase the carved whale I'm holding when my phone buzzes, drawing my attention away from the piece of art.

We've been contacted.

Viktor's message sends me out of the market and straight to the house. "Viktor?" I call, entering our home for the past three weeks. He steps out of a dark room, handing me my backpack. "We're leaving?"

"We're going to Jamaica."

the old amelia

JAMAICA IS close enough to Haiti that we're able to charter what I've heard called a "puddle jumper" to the island. I never understood the meaning of the word until riding inside one. I only thought the jet made me sick. Oh, my God, this is ridiculous. I'm taking a ship back to New Orleans.

I've never been so happy to see solid ground as we unload at the small airport. I resist the urge to kiss the concrete under my feet. Viktor hasn't said more than a few words since we boarded. So much for the "finding her together" portion of my speech from a few weeks ago.

"Are you going to tell me where we're going?" I ask, trailing behind him.

"I don't have a plan. We're supposed to wait to be contacted."

"That sounds fun," I answer sarcastically. "Let's get

a hotel and get cleaned up. I feel filthy after flying in that thing." I lead him to a hotel not far from the tiny airport. Not to my surprise, Viktor books two rooms. I don't bother to ask why, just take my key and head to my room. Why am I pissed? We were never a couple. We had sex once. Well, many times, but only on one night. That doesn't mean he's required to be with me or me with him. Right?

Unlocking the room, I'm enamored by the view in front of me. Aqua blue water covers as far as I can see through the glass doors that line the entire wall. "This is beautiful," I whisper to me, myself, and I. Choosing the bed closest to the water, I open the glass doors wide, allowing the breeze and smell of the ocean to waft inside. My phone buzzes several times. Pulling it out of my pocket, I don't bother to read the messages before turning it off and setting it on the bedside table.

Salt air fills my lungs as I watch several families enjoying the beach below. Watching them makes me miss my humanity. I miss baking my pasty white skin in the sun for hours only to peel and look the same afterward. The curse of a redhead is real.

I look at my reflection in the mirror. Sophie's right. Bright red roots are showing underneath the dark brown dye that I used as a disguise. I never thought I'd say this, but I miss my red curls. I grab my laptop from my backpack and head straight to Google to search for how to remove hair dye without damaging the hair. Apparently, all I have to do is have the old dye professionally stripped from my hair. One call to the salon on the first floor of the hotel and I discover they perform that very service and have an opening in an hour.

The process takes longer than I expected, but when the stylist turns me toward the mirror and I see my hair returned to normal, I can't control the tears that flow. "Are you not happy with our services, miss?" the stylist asks.

I grab his hand. "These are tears of happiness. I love it. Thank you so much!" I sign the ticket, charging the service, along with a huge tip to Viktor Luquire. Next door to the salon is a boutique, full of clothes I would never glance at in New Orleans. We're in Jamaica, and all bets are off. After trying on several items, I charge three outfits, two bathing suits, several pairs of shoes, and a large-brimmed hat to Viktor without blinking an eye. The sun has begun to set, and I feel more like myself than I have for a long time. Changing into one of my new outfits and styling my hair, I head downstairs to the bar.

It doesn't take long before someone approaches me. "Hello, beautiful." I turn, seeing a tall dark man with piercing brown eyes.

"Hello."

"How is someone so beautiful here alone?" He slides the stool next to me out. "May I?" I shrug without responding. He slides into the empty seat. "What are you drinking?"

"Blood," I answer, hoping he'll leave me alone.

"Sounds interesting."

I toast the air in front of him. "It is quite lovely." My drink isn't the blood my body craves, but a Bloody Mary drink that I'm not particularly enjoying at the moment.

"Two bloods, please," he asks the bartender. He holds his hand in my direction. "Jean-Luc. You are?"

"Amelia Lockhart," I answer truthfully.

"Amelia. Such a lovely name." The bartender sits a second drink in front of me. "You're American?"

"I am."

"What brings you to our beautiful island?"

"I came with a friend. He's here to meet with someone."

Jean-Luc takes a sip of his drink. "What a lucky man he is."

I pick up the new drink, tapping his. "My thoughts exactly." My phone has buzzed several times since being in the bar. I've ignored them all.

"Ah, there you are." Viktor moves to the other side of me. "I've been texting you."

"That was you? I didn't bother to check."

He looks me up and down. "I see you've had an eventful afternoon."

"Quite," I answer, doing my best to ignore him. "I'm having drinks with my new friend Jean-Luc." I point at Viktor. "Jean-Luc, this is my *friend*, Viktor."

Jean-Luc looks around me. "Viktor is who I'm here to meet with, actually. Had I known he had such a lovely companion with him, I would've arrived sooner."

"Of course, you're here to meet Viktor." I sigh, taking a sip of the alcohol. It tastes like toilet water, and I resist the urge to cringe at the flavor.

"Shall we?" Viktor asks, motioning toward a corner booth away from the crowd.

"Only if your lovely companion joins us."

"I would have it no other way," Viktor says, helping me off the barstool. I ignore his hand and jump on my own. The corner booth is round, and I slide to the middle, hoping to avoid both of the men.

"How may I help you, Mr. Luquire?" Jean-Luc asks, sliding into his spot in the booth.

"I've learned you are the one I need to speak to about immortal children," Viktor doesn't mince words.

"Immortal children?" Jean-Luc sounds amused at his question. "What is an immortal child?"

"I think you know. Are you going to help us, or not?"

"It depends."

"On what?" Viktor's face matches his voice. He's clearly in an amazing mood.

"On the reason for requesting such knowledge. You see, Mr. Luquire, I deal in truths. If you're not willing to share the truth with me, then I have no knowledge to bestow."

"One of my companions has learned of the possibility of an immortal child."

Jean-Luc slides off the bench. "Good evening, Mr. Luquire."

"For fuck's sake, Viktor." I touch Jean-Luc's hand.

"It's his daughter. Viktor's daughter is an immortal child. She's being hunted, and we need your help."

Jean-Luc slides back onto the bench. "There's the truth. Thank you, my dear." He takes a drink. "I believe I can help you."

"Has she contacted you?" Viktor asks.

"Your daughter? No. However, I am not the only one who has access to such knowledge."

"Then you're of no help to me." Viktor moves to slide out of the bench.

"What I *can* tell you is where she might be and what she's going through at the moment."

Viktor sits back down. "I'm listening."

"How valuable is this information to you?" Jean-Luc asks.

"If the information turns out to be legitimate, you can name your price." If I wasn't pissed at him at the moment, this would be kind of hot.

"I like the sound of that." Jean-Luc slides closer to me. "You're not very old, are you?" I don't answer. "Why are you here?" he asks. "What importance is this daughter to you?"

"She was my maker," I answer truthfully.

He laughs. "There it is. Not only do you have an immortal child for a daughter, but she's created another." He moves even closer. "I'm guessing the council has caught wind of her."

"Yes," Viktor confirms.

"Has he told you that his daughter's life isn't the only one in danger?" Jean-Luc asks me.

I turn toward Viktor. "What is he talking about?"

Jean-Luc laughs even louder. "You didn't tell her, my friend?" He turns toward me. "Not only will his daughter die at their hands, but so will you."

I stare at the man, replaying his words in my mind. I should've known that was a possibility, but the thought never entered my mind. "Excuse me, please." I move toward Viktor, trying to slide past him. He refuses to budge an inch. "Move, Viktor. Now."

He stays in place.

I switch into vampire mode and slide under the table at super speed and through the door before anyone notices. The night wind hits me, washing away some of the frustration I'm feeling at the moment. How could I be so naïve? I should've known I'd be killed too. She made me. An immortal child made me. Not only is she not allowed to live, neither is her creation. I move to the edge of the water, staring into pink, yellow, and blue hues as the sun sets in the sky.

"Celeste!" I call through my mind. *"Can you hear me?"* I'm met with no response. *"I need you right now."* I laugh at the irony of needing a five-year-old. Technically, and to the world around us, she should be the one needing me.

I sit on a large rock and watch the sun as it lowers completely into the sea. A flash of green happens just as the sun lowers. "Oh, my God," I say to no one. I've read about the green flare many times but never thought I'd witness one. Maybe that's the universe's way of telling me to quit feeling sorry for myself and get off my ass. My phone buzzes, and yet again, I ignore it.

The sun has completely set, and the light is nearly gone from the sky. A full moon rises, giving light where it was taken. My phone rings, startling me back to reality. No one ever calls me. I ignore it, sure Viktor is on the other end. It continues to ring five more times, and I ignore it all five times. The sixth time it rings, I answer. *"What, Viktor?!"*

"Amelia?" The voice on the other end is soft and vaguely familiar.

"Who is this?"

"Celeste."

I jump to my feet. *"Celeste? Where are you? Are you okay?"*

"I'm okay. I can't tell you where I am, but I will be home soon. You and Daddy need to go home to New Orleans."

"Celeste, they're after you."

"I know. You have to leave. You have to go home. Jean-Luc will lead you in the wrong direction."

"Celeste, how do you know we met Jean-Luc?"

"We're bonded, remember?"

"Viktor's not going to listen to me. Since you've been gone, he's in asshole mode." I stop, realizing what I just said. *"I'm sorry. I shouldn't say that about your father."*

She laughs softly. *"You're not telling me anything I don't know."*

"You have to talk to him. He won't listen to me."

"I can't. Our connection has been lost."

"Your connection to Viktor is lost? How?"

"I'll explain when I get home." Her voice sounds weaker than before. *"I need to go. Tell Daddy that when we lived in France, I had a hen that was my pet. The hen's name was Stubby, because she only had one foot. She laid the best eggs of any of the hens, and he would request his eggs, stubby side up."*

"What? What does that even mean?"

"Just tell him. He'll know you talked to me and will listen to you."

"Okay," I whisper. *"I love you, Celeste."*

"I love you, too." Her voice is barely audible as the phone goes silent. I turn, heading back into the hotel and the bar. The two men are still in the same spot, discussing who knows what.

"Ah, the lovely lady is back," Jean-Luc announces as I slide into the booth next to Viktor.

"I am. The sunset was lovely. It gave me a minute to think about everything, and I realized how much I miss food."

"I can help you with that, my dear." Jean-Luc smiles widely, giving me the creeps.

I turn toward Viktor. "You know what I miss the most? Eggs. Scrambled eggs were always my favorite." Viktor wrinkles his forehead, trying to figure out what I'm talking about. "Did you ever enjoy eggs?"

"Yes?" he answers, still confused.

"My favorite kind was stubby-side up." I laugh. "I mean, sunny-side up. That was a weird slipup." I stare into his eyes, begging him to understand. "Stubby-side up sounds like it could be from a one-legged hen." I see the moment Viktor makes the connection. His eyes change from confusion to comprehension.

He turns toward Jean-Luc. "Our conversation is over." He looks the man in the eyes. "You won't remember this conversation or meeting either of us." Jean-Luc's pupils enlarge, and his face becomes expressionless. "We've never met, and I do not have an immortal child. That would be breaking the rules, and I would never do that."

Jean-Luc closes his eyes while the two of us leave him alone in the booth. It's not until we're outside that Viktor stops me. "What's happened?"

"Celeste called me. She said her connection to you is lost but that Jean-Luc would lead us in the wrong direction. She said we need to go home."

"Go home? We're no closer to finding her than when we left."

"She said she'd explain everything when she gets home."

"Dammit. What do we do?" Viktor crosses his arms in front of his chest.

"We do what she says. We go to New Orleans."

lycanthrope protection detail

VIKTOR TAKES the puddle jumper back to Haiti and back to the private jet, while I choose a much slower, yet less nauseating mode of transportation—a boat. It's not until we're out of sight of land that I realize the boat is worse. The captain assured me his private vessel could easily make the distance between the two islands; however, he failed to mention the amount of bouncing we would do along the way. If vampires could turn green, I'm positive my coloring would match Shrek's.

I'm sitting below deck, hiding from the sun, and hoping the waves will be easier from here. They're not.

"Would you care for something to eat?" The captain's wife offers me something that looks like a biscuit.

"No, thank you. The only thing that would help right now is being on solid ground."

I slide back on the bench and close my eyes. Thoughts of Viktor and the way he's acted lately flood my mind. When I told him I'd rather take a boat, I expected him to come with me. To my surprise, he paid for the passage and left for the airport. We're not a couple, but now I'm not sure if we're even friends. Maybe I was nothing more than a one-and-done. Wham, bam, thank you, ma'am. Will he be waiting for me with the jet? The way things are going, no.

"We're docking soon, ma'am," a soft voice interrupts my thoughts.

I open my eyes to see the older woman hovering over me with yet another type of human food. "Thank you."

"Are you sure you wouldn't care for something to eat? Sometimes it can help ease the stomach."

I smile without answering and gather my bags. "How far is the airport from where we'll dock?"

"Not far. I'll call a taxi for you when we get there."

Heading up the narrow ladder to the top deck, I'm relieved to see the dock not far ahead. We're tied up within minutes, and then I'm walking the narrow wooden dock toward a gravel road. "There's the taxi now," the woman shouts as an older model car comes to a stop not far in front of me. I wave, thanking her for her hospitality.

"Airport, please." The driver spins out on the gravel, taking me away from one nausea-inducing item toward the next. My phone buzzes and reluctantly I pull it out. Right now, I don't want anything to do with Viktor.

> Heading back to New Orleans. I have another flight coming for you in three hours.

> Are you serious? Three hours? What am I supposed to do for three hours?

> Shop?

He sends a smiling emoji, and I throw my phone across the small car.

"Asshole," I whisper.

"Most are," my driver speaks for the first time. "I'm sorry. I didn't mean to eavesdrop."

"No, you're fine. I'm sorry to bring my drama into your car."

The man laughs. "If that's the least amount of drama I have today, I'm doing good." His accent has the perfect Southern gentleman charm to it. "The airport isn't much further."

"Actually, I just discovered I have three hours to kill. Is there anywhere close I can grab a drink?"

"I think I know the perfect spot." He turns the car in the opposite direction of the airport and parks in front of what looks like a hole in the wall.

"Is this a bar? It looks more like a dump."

He laughs. "I'll try not to take offense to that." He

steps out of the compact car, and to my surprise, he's at least six and a half feet tall. My door opens, and he offers me his hand. Standing in front of him, I realize the top of my head barely comes to his shoulders. "Topher." He holds his hand toward me.

"Topher? Is that your name?"

"It's a nickname. My name is Christopher, but my mom shortened it when I was a kid."

"Amelia," I answer, shaking his hand. "You're not bringing me here to kill me, are you?"

Topher laughs. "Nah, you're safe."

"All the same, I'd rather not be the only two people inside. You understand?"

He steps into the dim light hovering over the parking lot. Damn. Topher is hot. His shoulder-length dark brown hair is wavy and tied at his neck, while his emerald green eyes peer into my soul.

"I understand." He smiles. "I also understand that you are not a normal young woman." Dammit, why do I keep forgetting to hide my energy? I back away, ready to run. He holds his hands in front of him. "Don't go. I'm not here to hurt you." He looks around the empty parking lot. "My name is Topher St. James. I'm Edon's son."

"Edon? As in the Alpha of New Orleans, Edon? Why are you here?"

"My father, of course."

"Why would Edon send his son all the way to the

Caribbean for me? I don't need protection." I look into his eyes. "You know what I am?"

"I do."

"You know who I'm with?"

Topher looks around. "Um, no one."

I resist the urge to flip him off. "I mean, who I came to the island with."

"Yes. Viktor Luquire. He and my father have been acquaintances for a very long time."

"Then explain to me why Edon would send you here?"

He shrugs. "I don't question my father. However, I would imagine it has something to do with the fact that Viktor's not here with you and you throwing your phone across my backseat."

"So, are you my protector or something?"

He laughs. "I've never met a vampire who needed protection from a lycanthrope before. It was explained to me that I was here as an escort. Consider me your personal wolf companion."

"Like a dog?" I cross my arms at my chest. That was rude, and I don't care.

"Well, okay. If that's how you choose to think about it, then, like a dog."

"I'm sorry, that was a bitchy thing to say." I look at the creepy building in front of us. "Is this really a bar?"

Topher looks at the building. "On this island, probably."

"Why'd you bring me here?"

"I didn't want to lie to you, and you have three hours to spare."

"Are we just going to sit in a parking lot until time for my flight?" I lean against the car behind me.

"It's late. Nothing is open on the non-touristy side of the island until tomorrow. Abandoned parking lots are our only option."

Stepping away from the car, I sit on the edge of a broken curb, pulling my legs close to my body. "I knew your mother and brother."

"I know." He moves to the side of me, sitting a few feet away.

"She saved me. I didn't remember much about her until I became a vampire, then the memories of that time in my life came back to me. She was a wonderful woman."

"She was. Colby, on the other hand." He laughs at his words.

"Colby was my friend when I needed him."

"Yeah, he had a way of doing that. He was the baby of the family and got everything he wanted. Truthfully, he was a great man. I miss him."

"Me, too."

He turns toward me. "Why are you alone? I expected to have to explain why Edon sent me to Viktor. Did he leave you to fly home alone?"

I just met this man ten minutes ago. Spilling my entire life to him doesn't seem like the wisest choice.

"I'm not a fan of flying. He took an earlier flight rather than wait on my boat to arrive."

Topher shrugs, clearly not believing my story. "You're different from what I expected."

"What did you expect?"

He laughs. "I don't know. The few vamps I've met have been stiff, kind of jerks. You seem pretty cool."

"Ha. Give me a couple of centuries. I'm sure I'll be as stiff as the rest of them."

"Was the transition hard?"

"Yes and no." Again, I don't want to divulge personal information to a stranger.

"Turning into a vampire is different than being born into it like we are. We know from a young age what we are and what our limitations are." He jumps up, heading toward the car. "I have something for you." He comes back, carrying a bottle of red liquid. "I thought you might be hungry."

I take the bottle, not sure whether to trust him. He's right, I am hungry, but I still don't know this man. "Goat?"

"Of course. Only the best." He pauses. "You don't trust me, do you?"

"No."

"Call him. Call Edon." That's not a bad idea.

"Where would he be this time of night? He's not on speed my dial."

He smiles. "No, I'd imagine not."

Topher dials a number on his phone and hands it to me. "Hello?" a deep voice on the other end says.

"Hello?" I echo.

"Amelia?"

"Yes. Who is this?"

"Edon." I hand the phone back to Topher.

"Do I look like an idiot? I grew up in the projects of New Orleans, for God's sake. That could be anyone on the other end of the line. You can't seriously think I'd believe it's Edon." I grab my backpack, slam the car door behind me, and move away from the car.

"He wants me to tell you that I'm here, not only for protection but to be your friend." Tears stream down my eyes.

"That doesn't convince me that it's him," I yell across the parking lot.

"Edon says the pack has protected you since you were young and will continue to until we can't any longer. It's your choice whether you believe Topher is my son and sent by me but know we will be here for you."

I move across the parking lot at vampire speed, slamming him against the building behind us. To his credit, he doesn't fight back or even look scared. He towers over me. I look straight into his eyes, mimicking Viktor's move from earlier, and soften my voice. "Why are you here?"

"To protect you and be your friend," he whispers.

"Do you plan on trying to hurt me?"

"I'm here to protect you and be your friend," he repeats.

"Who sent you?"

"My father, Edon." I release the giant man, taking a few steps backward. It takes a few minutes for his eyes to return to normal.

"Did you just do something to me?" He rubs his eyes.

"No," I lie.

"Why do I feel weird?"

I shrug. "I'll take that goat blood now." He hands me the bottle, still looking around confused. I drink it in one gulp, grateful for the help.

"The sun is close to rising. Maybe we should head to the airport now." I nod, climbing back into the car. Watching him fold his body to fit inside is comedic. We don't speak on the way to the airport. No doubt, he's still feeling the aftereffects of the compulsion I forced on him. That was the first time I've ever used that technique, and to be honest, I'm surprised it worked.

We park in the small lot, and he follows me inside. "Why are you following me?"

"Maybe you misunderstood the protection and friend thing. Me coming with you is part of that deal." I stop walking.

"You're coming on Viktor's private jet, with me?"

The look he gives me reminds me of Colby. "Yes. Is that a problem?"

"Do I have a choice?"

"Nope," he answers, taking my backpack from me. "You're a feisty little thing, aren't you?"

team wolf

WE FIND a few chairs not far from the airport gate. Topher stretches his long legs in front of him and falls asleep on a chair that looks like it was made for a child. With the sun rising behind us, I take a minute to study the giant lycanthrope. His jawline is rigid and sharp, topped with high defined cheekbones with a small number of freckles scattered across his nose. He looks nothing like his parents or brother. I still don't trust him, but his tenacity is amusing.

"Miss Amelia Lockhart, please report to gate number seven," a voice sounds overhead. I kick his leg, trying to wake him.

He sucks in a quick breath. "What?"

"I think the jet's here."

He jumps to his feet. "Good. I'm ready for a seat that fits me." We walk to gate seven where an older woman greets us.

"Amelia Lockhart?"

"Yes, ma'am. That's me."

She takes a minute to look at the entirety of Topher. "And you are?"

"Christopher St. James. Miss Lockhart's companion."

"I'm sorry, sir. I don't have a record of a companion flying with Miss Lockhart today."

"Did I forget to put his name on the manifest?" Sophie comes out of nowhere. "How careless of me." She takes the paper away from the older woman and scribbles Topher's name across the top. "Here you go. Thank you for drawing that to my attention."

"Sophie!" I'm glad to see a familiar face.

"It's good to see you again, Miss Lockhart. Your plane is ready for boarding. Please follow me."

Once we're away from the gate, she turns with a smile. "It's good to see you, too. I'm sorry for the formality. I don't want that woman to suspect we're taking a strange man back to the States."

"Topher St. James." He holds his hand toward her.

"Aye, I remember. Sophie McKenzie," she answers. Shaking his hand. "Did you switch the grumpy one out for this hot one?" She nudges my shoulder with a laugh.

"There's no switching going on. This one is just following me."

Sophie turns, assessing the giant man behind me. "Aye, they tend to do that." We board the plane and are moving within minutes. "I brought you some Dramamine. It might help with nausea."

I don't have the heart to tell her that human medication won't affect me. I take the pills and smile. "Thank you, Sophie."

"You're welcome. I love your hair." She leads me to a seat toward the front of the plane. "The natural color suits you perfectly."

I run a hand through my curls, subconsciously. "Thank you."

"Don't you think so, Topher?"

He turns, smiling. "I didn't see the other color, but the red is perfect."

"Aye. Strap in, both of you. We'll be off the ground in minutes." Topher chooses a seat across from me. Close enough that we can talk, but far enough away that no one will mistakenly think we're a couple. I laugh at the irony. He's actually sitting closer than Viktor did on the way over here. Topher and I just met. Viktor and I have known each other for several years and have had sex.

Maybe it's the fresh goat blood, but liftoff doesn't send my stomach into my throat. This is much better than the last two experiences. As soon as the seatbelt light goes off, I unbuckle and turn toward my new friend. His legs are stretched across the aisle, making it nearly impossible for Sophie to pass the few times she does.

"You're blocking the aisle."

He slides his feet back, bringing his knees to the same level as his chest. "I'm sorry. These seats are not made for someone of your height. My fiancé and brother are about your size and have the same issue," Sophie says.

"Eh, I'm used to it. I've become a master at folding my legs."

"Or blocking the entire aisle."

"Or blocking the entire aisle," he echoes.

Sophie moves to the back of the plane, leaving the two of us alone. "Tell me about Topher, the lycanthrope."

He laughs. "Well, he's a great guy. He graduated top of his class, but being in the lycan business sort of put a damper on moving forward with his education."

"Why's that?"

"Being the oldest son of the Alpha leaves little room for job opportunities. I've been raised to take over my father's position since birth. That's my future job. It was decided long before me."

"That kind of sucks. You have no choice for your future."

"Do you?" he asks. Damn, that was harsh, and I don't answer. He slides his legs forward slightly and closes his eyes. He's right. I don't have any more of a choice than he does. I had no choice but to become the very thing that tried to kill me. The first vampire I had contact with turned out to be a psychopath and the second...well, the jury's still out.

The flight back to New Orleans is uneventful and quiet. Viktor hasn't texted, and I'm grateful. I'm not going back to Mandeville. I don't know where I'm going, but going back to that house right now isn't an option.

I give Sophie a quick hug and thank her for being so kind after the plane lands. Topher follows me off onto the tarmac. "Where are we going?" he asks, staying right on my heels.

I stop, turning to face him. "I don't know where you're going, but I know where I'm *not* going."

"Do you have anywhere you can go that doesn't involve Viktor?"

"No." My entire life rotates around him. How the hell did I do that? Celeste told me I had access to her money, but that means I have to contact Viktor, which is out of the question.

"You can come to my place."

"Topher, I don't think that's a great idea."

He holds his hands in front of him. "I don't mean anything inappropriate. I have an extra room that you are welcome to stay in."

"I barely know you."

"True, but you know my family."

"Okay. If this is some sort of setup, I will kill you."

"Consider me warned." He grabs my backpack. "My car is over here." I follow him to the parking lot and an older model Mustang.

"Is this your car?"

"It is. It used to belong to Edon. He passed it down to me not too long ago."

I slide into the glossy black sports car as the engine roars to life. Topher drives to a familiar part of town. "Are we heading to the Quarter?"

"I live off of Royal Street." Royal Street...this shit show has turned a complete circle.

"I grew up in the Quarter."

He pulls into a hidden driveway off Royal. A button on his sun visor makes what looks like a fence slide open and reveals a hidden parking lot. Inside there is room for at least ten cars. All spots are empty except for the one he parks in. "Home sweet home."

I follow him into the courtyard and up a narrow flight of stairs to the only door. The first thing I see inside the open room is an oversized pool table that sits in the middle of what is most likely the living room. A black sectional sofa sits facing the biggest television I've ever seen, hanging on an exposed brick wall. I don't know what I expected his home to look like, but this isn't it. In the back corner of the room is the kitchen. An island with four bar stools holds a sink and what looks like a dishwasher. An industrial-sized refrigerator sits across from it and is larger than the island. "This is really nice."

"Why do you sound surprised?"

"Because I am."

He leads me to a closed door in the opposite corner

of the kitchen. "I know vampires don't sleep, but this room is for you to use however you like."

I peek into the room. A king-sized bed sits against an exposed brick wall. The headboard is made from tufted navy blue velvet with bedding that matches. He flips a switch on the wall, and soft white LED lights glow from under the bed. "Did you decorate this?"

"I did. If you don't like it, keep it to yourself."

"It's beautiful. It looks professionally decorated."

Topher smiles. "Thank you, I think. Come to think of it, that's the first nice thing you've said to me."

"Yeah, well, don't get used to it." I resist the urge to smile. "Actually, thank you for this. You didn't have to open up your home for me."

Topher scoffs. "You're welcome. Make yourself at home. There's fresh goats' blood in the fridge." I turn toward my new friend, not sure what to say. My childhood and Harrison taught me not to trust so easily, but this wolf has been kinder than anyone in my life at the moment. He turns, leaving me alone in the room.

I throw my backpack and bag on the bed and plop down beside it with a thud. What are you doing, Amelia? What is your plan? I lay in silence waiting for someone to answer, disappointed when no answer comes. I pull out my phone, searching for a text that is not there. I sigh, sending one instead.

Back in New Orleans.

I swipe for what seems like hours on TikTok. I've cried, laughed, gone down three rabbit holes of conspiracy theories, and tried out at least ten new filters before my phone buzzes with a response.

> Good.

I stare at the word in front of me. Good? What the hell is wrong with him? Better yet, what the hell's wrong with me? Why do I fall in bed with the first man/vampire that shows me attention? What does that say about me? Now I'm in the home of a really hot lycanthrope and lying on one of his beds. Way to go, Amelia. Just try all the mythological creatures until you find one that doesn't try to kill you or ghost you. I laugh, remembering the popular vampire books I read in high school. I always was Team Wolf anyway.

My mind rambles through the insanity of my life until the sun is high in the sky. I sneak into the main room, finding Topher stretched out on the sectional. Why isn't he in his room? I search for a door that would lead to another bedroom, finding nothing. Did he give me his bedroom? I don't know whether to be pissed or think it's sweet.

I tiptoe past him to the gigantic fridge. He wasn't lying about it being stocked with blood. The door is full of bottles of blood, sitting next to bottles of beer. "Bit early for a drink, isn't it?"

I turn, finding the lycanthrope standing behind me. "Did I wake you?"

"Not really. I'm a light sleeper."

I grab a bottle of blood and move out of his way. "Did you give me your bed?"

"Maybe," he moves toward the fridge, grabbing an orange juice.

"Why'd you do that? I don't sleep. I would've been perfectly happy on the couch, staring at my phone, instead of your only bed, staring at my phone. You didn't need to give me your room."

Topher chugs the entire bottle of juice in one gulp. "I don't mind. Tonight, I might sleep on the pool table. Who knows?"

"That looks super comfy. Hopefully, tonight I won't be here. Today's plan is to find out where to go. Viktor owns properties all over the city. I'm sure there's one I can move into."

He makes a jump shot, hitting the trash can from across the room. "Suit yourself. The invitation to stay here is open. You're welcome anytime."

"You're not afraid I might drain your blood in the middle of the night?"

"It's a risk I'm willing to take." He scratches his head, making his hair frizz. "What are our plans for the day?"

"*Our* plans?"

"Yep. We're a package deal. You didn't realize that?"

"No...When did that happen?"

"You know how lost dogs are. When you find them, they're yours."

For the first time in a few days, I laugh. "In that case, *our* plan for the day is to find a place for *me* to live."

"I'm on it." He lifts his armpit, smelling under his arm. "I need a shower before we do anything."

"Yeah, me, too. However, that's not a 'we' thing."

It's Topher's turn to laugh. "After you, my lady." He motions toward the bathroom. "There are clean towels under the sink and shampoo in the shower. Help yourself to whatever you need."

"Topher, why are you helping me?"

"I told you. Edon..."

"I've known Edon for a while. Long enough to know that when he asked you to protect me, allowing me to sleep in your bed and use your towels wasn't what he was thinking."

He shrugs. "Maybe there's more of my mother in me than my father."

my new place

I DON'T KNOW why I bothered to look at my phone, there isn't a text from Viktor. There isn't a text from anyone, for that matter. I stare at the blank screen longer than I should, trying to decide if I should send him a good morning text. Thankfully, Topher exits the bathroom shirtless, wearing nothing but a pair of low-rise sleep pants, and distracts me from my insecurities.

"Give me a few minutes, and I'll be ready." He heads into the bedroom, holding my attention the entire way. *What are you doing, Amelia?*

Turning my attention back to my phone, I send a text to the only person I trust at the moment, Violet.

Hey!

Hey, yourself. What are you up to?

Violet sends a response instantly.

> Nothing and everything. I need a place to stay for a while. Any ideas?

> What's going on with Viktor?

I sigh before answering because I don't know what's going on with Viktor.

> I think it's better if we spend some time apart.

I choose the easy answer.

> I get it. You know you're always welcome here.

> I know, thx. But I want to be on my own. I need to figure this life out.

Violet takes longer to respond than earlier. I'm just about to slide my phone back into my pocket when it vibrates again. On the screen is a location marker.

> This house belongs to Viktor, but he never goes there.

> Think he'd want me to stay there?

> Do we care what he wants?

> No, we don't. Thank you.

Topher saunters his way back to the sectional. This time he's wearing a pair of tight-fitting jeans, boots, and a plaid button-down shirt. I swallow the lump that forms in my throat. Bella, you chose wrong, girl. Team Wolf is way hotter than Team Vampire has ever been.

"Find anything?" he asks, sitting a few cushions away.

"Maybe. A friend of mine sent me the location of a house that Viktor owns." I hand him my phone.

"That's not far from here. Let's go."

"There's a problem."

"You mean there's an opportunity?" he smiles. "At least that's what my mom always said."

"Well, our opportunity is I don't have access to the property, at least without asking Viktor."

"And, you don't want to ask him," Topher fills in the blanks.

"I don't want to talk to him right now. Let alone beg for a place to live."

"Beg? Who said anything about begging?" He pulls his phone out of the pocket that barely has room for a hand, let alone a phone. He pushes a few buttons before putting the phone to his ear. I stare at the giant in front of me. Is he calling Viktor?

"Hey, Dad." He smiles. "Yeah, I'm good. She's good, too." He winks at me with his words. "She needs a favor." He's quiet for a while, listening to whatever Edon is saying. "Of course," he answers. "She's safe. I'll make sure of it. She needs a place to stay. We have a location of one of Viktor's homes that he doesn't use. Do you think you can contact Viktor and get information on how to get inside?" Topher's listening intently to the voice on the other end. "Sounds good. Thanks. I'll let her know."

He hangs up the phone, and I stare at the giant in front of me, waiting on pins and needles. "Well?"

"He said he'd give him a call and let us know." He reaches a hand toward me. "In the meantime, let's go get something to eat and check it out."

"I already ate."

"Then you can watch me eat." When I don't accept his hand, he slides it back into his pocket.

"That sounds really exciting." I stand, barely coming to his pecs.

"Doesn't it, though?" His boots click across the concrete flooring as we head toward the door.

Typical French Quarter style, the streets are already full of tourists and leftover people from last night's party. We walk a few blocks to what looks like a small hole-in-the-wall. "This is where you want to eat?"

"Yep. Best biscuits in town."

"Looks like you're going to catch a case of crabs and cholera at the same time."

Topher laughs. "Wow. That's quite a load there. Crabs and cholera? What kind of service do you think they provide?"

"Topher!" an older woman greets us as we enter. "Back again?"

"You know it, Ms. Helen. You've got the best biscuits this side of the Mississippi."

"Damn right," she answers. "You want your usual?"

"Please."

"How about your friend? What would she like?"

"Oh, I'm good. I ate earlier."

Helen smiles. "Sure thing, baby. Topher, yours will be right out."

I pull my phone out, searching for directions again. "It looks like the house is not far from here. I grew up in the Quarter, but for some reason, I can't picture this location."

"We'll check it out when we leave." Topher's energy is easy and relaxed. After living with vampires for nearly two years, I'm grateful.

"Here you go, honey." Helen sets down at least ten plates, each full of different breakfast food.

"Is all that for you?"

"I'm a growing boy." He laughs.

"You're out of room to grow."

"Nah. There's always room. In fact, by the time I become Alpha, I'll probably grow a few more inches."

"Seriously?"

"Seriously." He's emptied three of the plates in front of him already. "The Alpha has to be larger than anyone else. It keeps them from being challenged."

"Edon has to die for you to become Alpha? Right?"

"That or I challenge him for the title."

"Is that something you've thought about?"

Topher laughs. "No. If I had my way the title would be passed down to one of my brothers." His phone buzzes, vibrating the table. "Speak of the devil. Edon has talked to Viktor and is going to send the code to get inside the house." I sigh in relief. "Viktor's going to have your things sent over."

"So that's it?"

He stacks the empty plates in front of him. "How long have you two been together?"

I can't hold back the inauspicious laugh. "Together isn't a word I'd use to describe whatever we were." I slide back into the booth. "We were never a couple in the true sense of the word. Honestly, I don't know what we were or are. I don't even know anymore."

"Don't take this the wrong way, but the less vampires, the better."

"Not a fan?"

"Not particularly. You're okay, though." He lays a twenty-dollar bill on the table before standing. "Keep the change, Ms. Helen. It was delicious, as always."

"Thank you, baby. I'll see you again tomorrow." She waves as I follow him out of the tiny restaurant.

Three blocks later, we stop in front of what looks like an empty warehouse. "Is this it?" I check my maps three times before deciding that this is the correct location.

Topher pulls a tall bush away from what looks like an abandoned door to find a hidden keypad. He enters a code from his phone, and the door pops open. "This is it."

We enter a room with nothing on the walls or floors. Perfectly stained concrete leads to a set of stairs in the back of the room. Topher steps in front of me, leading the way. I laugh at the irony. "You do know I'm a vampire, right?"

"Yep."

"I don't need you to protect me." He doesn't answer, just continues to lead the way up the winding staircase. The stairs lead to what looks like a flat ceiling. "What the hell?"

"There has to be a door here." He pushes slightly on the ceiling, looking for a way inside. I hear a soft click, and he releases a hidden latch. "Found it." He pushes the door open, revealing a loft apartment and exposed brick. "Holy shit. This is nice."

I follow him inside and am shocked at what awaits. The layout is similar to Topher's loft with one large room. Unlike Topher's loft, this one has been professionally decorated. Greenery hangs around the room, bringing the room to life. Light flows through the oversized windows, providing warmth and comfort. "I love it." The words whisper from my lips.

"Me, too. I may move in." He laughs.

In the back corner sits a large bed with soft white bedding. The living area is home to a white sectional sofa, facing a television that rivals Topher's in size.

"This doesn't look anything like Viktor's other properties."

"Dad said your items should be delivered by noon. In the meantime, why don't we watch a movie?"

I turn toward the lycanthrope. "A movie?"

He shrugs. "Why not? This television is larger than some movie screens. We might as well put it to use."

"O...okay," I stutter. He's right. What else is there to do? Celeste is nowhere to be found. Viktor and I are...I don't know what we are. There's an ancient vampire council that wants both me and Celeste dead. Watching a movie is a brilliant idea. "I'm in."

Topher props his large feet on the table in front of the couch and turns the television on. "Look at that. It's already loaded with every streaming service known to man."

"This does not feel like something Viktor would do. I'm not sure he even knows what a streaming service is."

He shrugs. "Maybe he had help." He flips through several of the services before settling on a movie that makes me laugh.

"Really? We're going to watch *Twilight*?"

"Yes! What's wrong with it?"

"Nothing. It's just a little ironic, don't you think?"

"That's the beauty of it. We can laugh at the misconceptions together."

I try to prop my feet beside his, my toes barely touching the edge of the table. "Bring it."

We watch the first and part of the second movie before someone rings a doorbell below. "I bet that's your stuff."

We head downstairs, and I instantly feel Viktor. "Shit," I whisper. "Go back upstairs."

"Are you sure?" I nod, and he heads to the top of the spiral staircase, as I move toward the door.

I take a deep breath before opening the heavy door. "Viktor?"

"Amelia." He looks down as he speaks. "I brought a few suitcases with your clothes." I look past him at the designer bags, full of clothes I didn't buy. "Your car should be delivered this afternoon."

"What the hell's going on, Viktor?"

He finally looks me in the eyes. "I'm sorry, Amelia."

"So, this is it? I get the fact that you don't want a relationship with me, but I thought we were friends. What happened to that?" I fight the tears threatening to fall.

"We were, we *are* friends. I just can't think of anything else besides Celeste right now. She's my priority."

"You don't think she's mine? She's my maker. I want her safe just as badly as you do. Pushing me away isn't going to bring her back any sooner."

He hands me an envelope before turning to leave. "Goodbye, Amelia." What in the ever-living hell? He jumps into an awaiting SUV parked illegally on the curb and speeds off. I stare at the back of the car, not sure what just happened.

I drag the suitcases up the winding stairs and toward the lycanthrope waiting at the top. "Are you okay?"

"I don't know," I answer truthfully. "I think maybe we just broke up. But I'm not sure we were ever dating. In other words, I don't know."

Topher takes the suitcases, carrying them toward the bedroom corner. "I've never been a huge fan of Luquire, so my opinion won't help. Instead, I vote we finish movie number two. Bella's got to get out of her funky mood eventually."

"Spoiler alert..."

"Shh, don't tell me."

"Have you truly never seen the movies or read the books?"

"Nope. What's that?" Topher points at the envelope Viktor handed me before leaving.

"Viktor gave it to me."

"Want me to put it with the rest of your stuff?"

I nod, handing it to him. I don't want to know what's inside. At least, not right now. "Then, we can finish watching Bella sulk."

allegiance of protection

"THAT'S NOT HOW IT WORKS," Topher announces as the credits roll.

"How what works?"

"The whole wolf transition thing. We don't just switch from one to another that quickly. It's a painful process that feels like every bone in your body is breaking at the same time."

"That sounds like loads of fun. If it makes you feel better, the vampire stuff wasn't accurate either."

"You don't glisten in the sunlight?"

I laugh, remembering this exact conversation I had with Harrison a lifetime ago. "Not that I've noticed."

"Are you happy being a vampire?" I look at my hands, suddenly feeling awkward.

"To be honest, I don't have anything to compare it to."

"Are you telling me you've never been happy?"

"My life has never been easy. I pretty much raised myself. Becoming a vampire was the first time I felt like I had a family."

"Family's not all it's cracked up to be."

"That's easy for you to say. Your mom was amazing, and your dad is pretty cool." I remember the kind nurse that helped me when I was sixteen. "She helped me when no one else would."

"Yeah, she was like that. She'd give you the shirt off her back if you needed it. I miss her." His voice sounds sad.

"My mom was crap. She left me alone most of the time, and by the time I turned twelve, she stopped coming home at all. I found out later she was one of Harrison's donors."

"Chamberlin? That guy was a creep." That's an understatement. Topher claps his hands loudly. "I'm hungry. My breakfast has deserted me." He changes the subject, and I'm grateful.

"The sun is starting to set. Let's go for a walk and make fun of tourists."

"I like how you think. Can I get some food while we're out?" He walks to a door on the other side of the room and pushes a button. A soft ding echoes off the walls and the door slides open.

"An elevator? There's a freaking elevator in here?"

"Most of these old lofts have one. How do you think they got the furniture up here? It certainly didn't come up the spiral stairs." I follow him onto the large freight elevator, and he slides the wall back in place. "It's left-over from when this was an actual warehouse." He pushes the down button, and we lower to the bottom floor. Instead of the entrance foyer we came through, we exit the building into a beautiful courtyard, typical of New Orleans. The courtyard opens straight onto Bourbon Street, and as I suspected, the street is full. Most are already wobbly as they jump from building to building, bar to bar.

We barely make it fifty feet before a large man steps in front of us. "What are a wolf and bloodsucker doing together?"

I recognize him instantly. "Drew, my friend. How are you?"

"I'm not your friend, leach."

"I see you're still full of personality. How'd the whole cult thing work out?"

"Shut up, bitch."

Topher steps between me and the lycanthrope. "You'll do well remembering who you're speaking with."

"Are you threatening me, *Christopher*?"

"No, *Andrew*. I'm not. I'm simply helping you to remember your place." Topher's voice is smooth and calm.

"My place? Who do you think you are? You're nothing more than an Alpha wannabe, following in his daddy's shoes. You haven't had to fight for anything in your life, Mama's boy."

Topher's hand changes into a claw as he wraps it around Drew's neck. "I suggest you shut your mouth while you still have the ability to breathe."

"Whatever," Drew spews, pulling away from Topher's grip and continuing down the street. Topher watches him until he's out of sight.

"Asshole," he mumbles. "Sorry about that."

I scoff. "Don't apologize for him. He's the product of bad breeding. I've had the pleasure of meeting him on several occasions." Topher's hand changes back to normal in an instant. "I thought you said it was painful to switch?"

He wiggles long, human-shaped fingers in front of his face. "It is, but sometimes it's necessary. Now, I'm *really* hungry."

"I know a place. What day is today?"

"Thursday. Why?"

"Trust me." I lead him off of Bourbon to a back alley that leads to what was one of my favorite places when I was human. Hopefully, Thursday hasn't changed locations. We round the corner of Toulouse Street, and the top of the cart umbrella comes into view.

"A hot dog cart? You're bringing me to a hot dog cart?"

"Not just a hot dog, my friend. New Orleans's best hot dogs. In fact, they're said to be the best hot dogs in the world."

"Who says that? The owner of the cart?"

"Maybe. Come on, you're going to love them. I can

watch you eat and remember the joy they would bring me when I managed to scrape up enough money to buy one." I grab his elbow, dragging the giant down the street.

"Amelia?" the older man says as we walk up. "It's been ages since I've seen you. You look wonderful!" He walks around the cart and hugs me. "You look... healthy."

"I am, Mr. Johnson. Thank you. I brought my friend to try one of your world-famous dogs."

"Now you know, no one can eat just one. Judging by his size, he's going to need at least three of them. What would you like on them, son?"

"Chili and jalapeños, please." I resist the urge to cringe at his toppings.

"Sure thing. Amelia? You want yours dressed like usual?"

"Oh, not today. Make mine the same as his. That sounds good." Actually, it sounds like ass, but I don't want to burst his bubble.

Mr. Johnson hands me five hot dogs, and I realize I don't have any money to pay for them. Topher hands him a twenty-dollar bill with a smile. "Thank you, sir. These look amazing."

"It's good to see you again, Amelia. Come see me when you can."

"I will. Thank you again, Mr. Johnson." We walk away in silence, heading toward the square. Memories of Harrison and Viktor come to mind as we pass the vendors and head toward the grassy area. Topher holds the gate into the picnic area open wide, waiting for me to enter.

"Do you mind if we go somewhere else?" I look toward the spot where Harrison and I shared our first picnic. "This place holds memories I'd rather not be reminded of."

"Sure. How about we go to the river?"

"Better." I smile.

We find an empty bench, and Topher has three of the hot dogs eaten within minutes. "I think you're right. These are the best hot dogs in the world."

"See, I told you. Mr. Johnson gave me food without charging me on more than one occasion. He kept me from starving a few times." It's at this moment an epiphany hits me. My entire life has been lived from one rescue to another. When I didn't have food, someone would take care of me. When I had dirty clothes and no water, someone bought me clothes and turned my water back on. Even now, people are saving me. What the hell? It's time to step up and save myself.

"What are you thinking?" Topher asks, finishing off the last hot dog.

"I'm thinking I've spent my entire life waiting for someone to rescue me when all the time the only person who can rescue me is me."

He wads the papers into a small ball. "That was kind of deep. Where do we start?"

"What?"

"Where do we start rescuing you?"

"*We* don't start anywhere. You see, that's the problem. I need to do it on my own."

He stands, patting his stomach. "I'm full. I need to go meet with Edon. Would you like to come, or will you be too busy solving your problems yourself?"

"I can spare a few hours." Topher leads me away from the river and toward a very familiar bar. "Is this where Edon is?"

"Yes. If you're worried about the lycan inside, they won't bother you. You're with me. I'll protect you...I mean, you can protect yourself. I'll just watch."

Memories of this building sit on the cusp of my mind. "I've been here before."

"You've been to a lycan bar?"

"I'm not sure. Something about this feels familiar. Maybe your mother brought me here?" He looks around the dimly lit room.

"She brought a teenager to a bar? Sounds about right." He laughs.

"There's the office." I point to a door leading to the office.

"That's the Alpha office."

I follow him into the familiar room. Edon stands the moment we enter. "Amelia!" he rushes to the other side of the desk, wrapping long arms around my shoulders. "It's good to see you. How are things?"

"I'm good, thank you."

Edon pats Topher on the shoulder, giving him the half-man hug. "I see you've met my son, Christopher."

"I did."

"Have a seat, please." He motions toward a set of matching chairs in front of the desk. "How did everything work out with the new apartment?"

"It's more than I could've hoped for. Thank you for arranging that."

Edon smiles. "Viktor was more than happy to offer the home. I'm glad you were able to get settled in." He leans back in the desk chair, propping his feet in front of him. "We have word that a member of the council is in town. Is this true?"

I don't know how to answer. Honestly, I don't know who to trust anymore. Looking around the remodeled office, memories flood my mind. Edon's wife...Topher's mother saved me. The lycan have been the one consistent thing in my life since I can remember. They've never hurt me or tried to scare me. In fact, they've done the opposite. I clear my throat and square my shoulders. "Yes. That's true. Her name is Hypatia, and she's both Harrison's and Viktor's maker."

Edon sighs deeply. "Why is she here?"

I look at my knees. "Celeste."

"Dammit." Edon stands, walking to a window on the other side of the room. "They'll want her dead."

"What am I missing?" Topher asks, looking between the two of us.

"Celeste is an immortal child. She's against the rules."

Topher turns toward me. "An immortal child? As in a kid vampire?"

Edon turns back in our direction. "Immortal children are against the rules in their world. The children are deadly and unpredictable."

"Celeste isn't any of those things. She's brilliant, kind, loving, and in complete control." The memory of her becoming a monster and killing the strigoi flashes to mind. I keep the memory to myself.

"She's a child vampire?" Topher repeats.

"She's over seven hundred years old but looks like she's five," I answer.

"Am I the only one that thinks that's sad?" Topher slides to the front of his seat. "I can't imagine being trapped in the body of a preschooler for that amount of time."

"Hypatia gave Viktor three months."

"Before they kill her?" Edon asks.

"To turn her into the council." My voice sounds sad.

"No wonder Luquire's been out of reach. His only option is turning his child over to die."

I sigh. "Celeste is missing."

"What do you mean, missing?" Edon steps away from the window.

"I mean she's not in New Orleans. She's gone."

"Desperate people will do desperate things. I don't blame him for trying to protect his daughter."

I stand, moving to the other window. "Viktor doesn't know where she is. That's why we went to Haiti. She's trying to find something that will help her grow. Phillipe heard rumors of practitioners in the islands that could help. We went searching for answers."

"Did you find any?" Topher asks.

"Yes and no." I turn toward the two men. "Celeste hadn't been there, but we did find an immortal child who had grown."

"Grown? Are you trying to tell me a vampire aged?" Topher looks confused by his question.

"That's exactly what I'm trying to tell you."

"How?" Edon asks.

"A spell."

Edon sits back at his desk. "Celeste is trying to age herself." He connects the dots.

"If she's not a child, the council won't have any reason to kill her...or me."

Topher slides his hands into his pockets. "Why would the council want to kill you?"

"Because Celeste is my maker." Both lycan stare at me blankly.

"I always thought wolves had the most drama. Now, I'm not convinced." Topher's words make me laugh.

"What happens if Celeste doesn't return in three months?" Edon asks.

I shrug. "I'd assume Viktor and I would be killed. You know, an eye for an eye type thing."

"He's not going to give her up, no matter the consequence. Even if she shows back up tomorrow, he's not going to let Hypatia have her." Edon's right. No matter what I thought I meant to Viktor, his daughter's life comes first. He's going to protect her with his life.

"There has to be another answer," Topher says.

"I've spoken with Celeste a few times. She says she's close to figuring it out."

"How the hell can we depend on a five-year-old to figure anything out?" he retorts.

"She may be five years old on the outside, but she's a seven-hundred-year-old genius on the inside."

Edon slaps a folder on top of his desk. "While you're both here, we have something else to worry about—the cult."

I plop back into the chair. "I thought we got rid of them."

"You got rid of Greg, but a new leader has stepped up." He hands me the folder. "They've been meeting in secret and have moved out of the Quarter."

"This is getting better by the moment," Topher announces.

"Do we know who this new leader is?" I flip through the pages, stopping at a familiar face. "Roger? Is this Roger?" I hold the picture for both of them to see.

"He goes by *Angel of Death*, but yes. His real name is

Roger Smith, and he's barely nineteen years old. Do you know him?"

"Sadly. I knew him as a confused college freshman. The Roger I knew was too busy trying to fit in to be the head of a cult. Are you sure he's the leader?"

"Our informants say yes."

"Unless he's had a major transformation, Roger's nothing to worry about. Our biggest concern is the council." I throw the folder back on Edon's desk.

"I hope you're right. What can we do about the council situation?"

"Until we know where Celeste is, nothing," I answer truthfully.

"Viktor's not going to let the council get that far. He's going to protect her with his life." Edon's words mimic my thoughts.

"He's going to get himself killed along with who knows how many others," Topher states the obvious. "He's no match for the council. If he tries to stop them, he'll bring their wrath on the entire city."

"Celeste is our only answer. We have to find her." Edon stands from his desk.

"We tried that. She'll find us when she's ready." I stand, heading toward the door. "I won't allow you to hurt her." I look both men in the eyes. "Do you understand?"

"We do," Edon answers for both of them. "I can assure you that won't be a problem. We are sworn to protect you and the ones you love."

I turn, leaving the office and the bar. I don't know if Topher is behind me, but don't turn to find out. What did Edon mean they're sworn to protect me? Was that common verbiage? Who would they even swear their allegiance to? I walk several blocks back to my new apartment and enter the code. As soon as the door pops open, I move vampire speed inside and straight to the envelope Viktor handed me this morning.

Unfolding the stack of papers, the first thing I see is a check with so many zeros on it, I have to count them five times. What the hell? Behind the check are deeds to this property and four more located throughout the Quarter, along with several stocks and bonds certificates. The last item in the stack is a handwritten note with three simple words.

Amelia, forgive me.

going on a quest with a lycan

FOR THE FIRST time in a few days, I'm alone and don't know what to do with myself. I've spent the past few hours organizing my clothes and arranging them in a closet that's bigger than the entire apartment I grew up in. Several times I've had my phone in my hand, one button away from texting Viktor, but stopped myself before hitting send. If he wants to contact me, he will. This afternoon's conversation plays through my mind on repeat. Between the cult and the council, we're fucked.

My phone buzzes, drawing me back to the present.

> I'm bored. Wanna watch the third movie?

I stare at the text.

> Topher?

The one and only.

Did I give you my number?

I know good and well, I didn't.

No, but I'm smart.

Edon had it, didn't he?

Maybe...

Sure, come on over.

Less than a minute later, the doorbell rings. "That was fast." I open the door and find him leaning against the brick facade, wearing sweatpants and a hoodie. "Are you planning on staying the night?"

"Is that an invitation?" He wiggles his eyebrows as he speaks.

"Nope. Not an invitation. Jumping into bed with another mythological creature is at the bottom of my to-do list. I'm swearing off all vampires and lycan."

"Good thing I'm just here to watch a movie, then. I changed into my comfy clothes, though." He follows me up the metal staircase and into the open loft apartment. "This is a really cool place."

"Yeah, I agree. Viktor gave me the deed, so it's officially mine."

"That's awesome. Congratulations." He moves to

the couch, picking the side closest to the television. "Bella needs to make a choice, either Team Wolf or Team Vampire. She can't have the best of both worlds."

I laugh, sitting on the other end. "What's wrong with having both worlds? I'm a vampire, being protected by werewolves. And why is that, by the way? Why am I being protected by wolves? Your dad said you made an oath to protect me and the ones I love. Why and to whom?"

"Did he say that?" I stare at the lycanthrope at the other end of the couch without answering. He relents with a shrug. "It had something to do with my mother."

"Why?"

"I don't know why. Are we going to watch Bella and the Big Bad Wolf, or not?"

"Not until you tell me why."

He turns, sliding a leg beside him. "I'm not lying when I say I don't know. Edon never told me why, just that I was to protect you. My father is the Alpha of New Orleans. I grew up learning not to question him."

"I don't need your protection."

"Then, I'm here to watch Bella make dumb choices, not to protect you."

I turn, facing the television. "Fair enough."

Topher flips through Netflix and starts the movie, stopping it after the first scene. "What the hell? Is that how it happened to you? That guy Riley was minding his own damn business, and the next thing he knows, he's a vampire."

"Not quite. Honestly, I don't know all the details of making a new vampire, but I know that's not how it works. And no, that's not how it happened to me." He pushes play, and we finish the movie without any more disruptions until we get to the end. Topher stares at the screen blankly. "What the hell? After all that, she chose the vampire. She's going to marry him?"

"I'm guessing you're still Team Wolf?"

"Yes! I can't believe she chose the one who broke her heart. I don't know if I want to watch the next movie."

"Spoiler alert, Jacob imprints on the baby. Actually, he doesn't imprint on her until the last movie."

He turns his large body completely toward me. "He what?"

"He imprints on the baby," I repeat. "Doesn't your pack imprint on future mates?"

"I'm guessing since I don't know what that word means, it's not something we do regularly."

"Imprinting is when your future mate is chosen for you. It's like love at first sight but on a molecular level." I can't help but laugh at the look on Topher's face. It's a mixture of disgust and intrigue.

"He imprints on an infant?"

"How does your pack choose their mates?"

Topher shrugs. "Tinder, Grindr...I don't know."

"Is there a special lycan app?"

"No, but you may be on to something." He pauses. "My parents were fated mates."

"What does that mean?" I turn, completely facing him.

"Pretty much like it sounds, a couple that's fated to be together. My parents were very much in love. Her death was hard on him."

"How did she die?" I remember my high school principal telling me the nurse had been found dead but never knew any details.

He looks down, picking at a stray string attached to his pants. "She was murdered."

"Do they know what happened?"

He shakes his head. "No." He doesn't elaborate, and instead of pushing him, I change the subject.

"Tell me more about fated mates. It sounds interesting."

"There's not much to tell. It's an old tradition. My parents were the only fated mates for the past hundred years, and there haven't been any since." He shrugs.

"Is it an Alpha thing?"

"Maybe? Although, that would mean there's a mate somewhere out there for me. That's weird to think about."

"Hopefully, she likes to cook." Topher laughs at my words. "Feel like watching the next movie?"

"Ready and willing." He flips to movie number four and pushes play.

Not long after the opening credits roll, I hear soft snores coming from the other side of the couch. His eyes are closed, and his mouth is open. Grabbing a fluffy pink blanket off the back of the couch, I cover him as much as possible before heading to bed and doing something I haven't done in a long time—read.

The night passes quickly, and my nose stays buried in books until the sun rises. Turns out vampire speed not only applies to my movement but also to reading. No wonder Celeste can devour an entire subject in an hour. In the time that Topher's been asleep on my couch, I've read an entire four-book series and am about to start a new one. My phone rings, drawing me out of the world of fae and back to reality. I don't recognize the number but answer anyway.

"Hello?"

"Amelia?" The voice on the other end isn't one I recognize.

"Yes, who's speaking?"

"It's me, Celeste." I stare blankly at the phone.

"Celeste? Why do you sound like a grown-up?"

"Because I am," she answers. I can tell she's smiling on the other end of the line. I don't know what to say and am not convinced this is really Celeste.

"Tell me something that only Celeste would know."

A soft laugh comes through the phone. *"I tricked you into letting me fly on a kite when we first met."*

"Celeste? Is it really you?" my voice cracks.

"It is." I can't stop the tears from flowing.

"I've missed you."

"I miss you, too. There's so much to tell you."

"Are you coming home?"

"Yes. Soon," she answers. I hear a deep voice in the background but can't understand their words. *"I have to go. I'll be in touch."* She hangs up before I can say anything else.

I move across the loft to the couch where Topher is still sound asleep. The blanket I placed on top of him has fallen to the side, and his hoodie has risen on his chest, exposing the beginning of a six-pack of abs. I resist the urge to follow the goodie trail any lower.

"Like what you see?" a sleepy voice whispers.

I clear my throat. "Nope." I kick his long legs. "Get up. You're snoring."

He stretches, holding his hands high above his head. He looks at least seven feet tall from fingertips to toes. "What did you do all night?" he asks.

"I visited the world of fae."

"Are they real too?" He laughs as he speaks.

"Probably. Although, there was a very hot fae in the series I read that I wouldn't mind if he were real." I kick his legs again. "I read for the first time in a while last night."

"Books?"

"No, I read the backs of all the boxes and items in the cabinets all night long." I give him a stupid look. "Of course, it was books."

"I was about to ask how much MSG is in a box of rice."

I can't help but smile. "You're a jerk."

"Me the jerk? You need to look in the mirror." He stops stretching, looking at me suddenly. "Do you have a reflection? Can you see yourself in a mirror?"

"That's a myth. I do indeed have a reflection."

"Good to know." He stands, towering over me. "Did you finish the movie without me?"

"Nah, I knew you'd want to sit through the torture of their honeymoon adventures with me." I pause. "Celeste called me."

"Celeste? Are you okay?" he asks, sitting back on the couch.

"I am. She didn't sound the same."

"What was different?"

"She sounded like an adult."

"Do you think she found something that made her grow?" He folds the blanket, placing it back on the couch.

"Maybe. She hung up before I could get any more information or tell her anything about what was going on here."

"Did she say when she was coming back?"

"Soon. I don't know anything else. That's all she said before she hung up."

He stands, moving toward the window overlooking Bourbon Street. "What are *we* doing today?"

"Don't *you* have something to do?"

"Yes. Hanging out with you. You're my mission."

"I don't need a babysitter," I remind him.

"Fully aware. Just here to hang out."

"Topher, you've barely left my side since Jamaica. I'm not convinced that you're doing this just because your dad, the big, bad Alpha asked you to."

"Edon told you, my family is sworn to protect you."

I sit on the couch. "Why, Topher? Why are they protecting me?"

"I'm not lying when I say I don't know. My mother insisted we swear an oath, and we did." A memory sits on the cusp of my mind. Not quite there but familiar all the same. "Why does your face look like that?" he asks.

"Remember when I told you I barely have memories of your mother other than she helped me when no one else would?" He nods. "I feel like most of my memories from that time were taken away. I know that sounds crazy, but I don't know how else to describe it."

"It doesn't sound crazy. We're mythological creatures, remember? Nothing sounds crazy anymore. Maybe your memory was wiped."

"Like a spell or something?"

He moves back across the room. "It's possible. I know just who to ask." He heads toward the elevator. "Coming?"

I don't ask questions and follow him down the stairs. Parked inside the parking area in the courtyard are my red BMW and my ancient Nissan. "Looks like my cars were delivered."

Topher steps back, staring at the two choices.

"Nothing against that little Nissan, but I vote we take the BMW." We climb inside and turn onto the busy street.

"Where are we going?" I ask.

"Algiers."

secrets are revealed

NOT LONG AFTER, we cross the CCC Bridge, heading toward the quieter part of New Orleans. Topher steers me into an older neighborhood not far from the bridge. The homes are shotgun style and painted bright colors, giving them a Rainbow Row look.

"Park in front of that one." Topher points to a small chartreuse-colored home on the right side of the street.

"Who lives here?"

"A friend of mine." The yard is perfectly manicured, and the turquoise door and shutters are the perfect match for the color.

"This is cute." I follow him to the brightly colored front door. Topher rings the bell, which surprisingly sounds like a foghorn.

"Topher?" an older voice says through the peephole. The door opens wide, revealing an older dark-skinned man. He's no taller than me and appears to be in his late '80s. "What are you doing here, boy?"

"Hello, Mr. Sam. You look older than the last time I saw you." My eyes widen at his words. *There are some things we don't say out loud, Topher.*

"You look hairier than last I saw you," Mr. Sam retorts. The two men laugh before embracing. "Who is the lovely vampire you've brought to see me?"

Topher steps aside. "Mr. Sam, this is Amelia."

"Hello, beautiful Amelia." Sam takes my hand into his, kissing it seductively.

"Don't get any bright ideas, Sam. We're here for purely platonic reasons." What the hell? I have a running list of questions building in my head.

"Come in." He steps out of the doorway, making room for us to enter. The inside is as perfect as the outside. The Victorian furniture looks to be original to the home and looks like it just came off the showroom floor. The walls are painted a soft lime green, which in the suburbs would be hideous. However, in this home, they're perfect. "Can I get you anything to eat or drink?" He looks at me with his last words.

"No, thank you." I smile.

"Mr. Sam. We're here for more...medicinal purposes."

Sam sits on the perfect couch. "Okay, son. What do you need?" Topher looks at me. Apparently, it's my turn to talk.

I take a deep breath, not sure how to start. "I'm a young vampire."

"Oh, I could tell that the moment you stepped out of that fancy car out there." He smiles.

"Most of my memories came back when I was changed, but there's a part of my life that I think was erased from my mind."

Sam sits back on the couch. "How so?"

"When I was in high school, I had a rough go of it. I was living on my own in Calliope and terrified."

"Calliope? That place was rough. Thank goodness the city shut it down."

"Agreed. Long story, short, Topher's mom saved me. She helped me when no one else would. I'm not sure how to explain it." I sigh before continuing. "She helped me because she could see through my farce."

"Cherie always was one of my favorites. I miss that girl." Topher looks down at Mr. Sam's words.

"I know there was more to the story than her helping me because of her job. A memory or something similar is on the edge of my mind, almost like it's on a cliff, about to fall off, but not quite there."

"Could your memory have been cleansed?" Sam asks.

"Maybe? I don't know. It's so familiar, yet not, at the same time." I laugh awkwardly. "It sounds dumb to say out loud."

Sam gets up, heading toward a curtain against the wall. He slides it open, revealing an altar of sorts.

"There's an easy way to find out." He starts mixing different powders in one container and liquids in another. A few minutes later, he stands in front of me with one in each hand.

"What is that?" I ask.

"It's a memory powder. If your memory was wiped through magic, this will do the opposite. If it wasn't wiped, you won't notice anything."

"What's the liquid for?"

He lifts the liquid to his lips, emptying the glass. "It's vodka." He smiles a wicked smile.

"Are you okay with this?" Topher asks beside me. I nod.

"Tell me what…" Sam blows the powder into my face, and my world goes black.

Visions of a vampire with long hair tied at his neck flash to mind, sitting on the couch of my childhood apartment. The image switches to Cherie, Topher's mom. She smiles warmly at me, helping me find clothes that fit my undernourished body. They have the same eyes. My memory switches to my apartment and the new couch that she bought me.

"I would like to know why the wolf population of New Orleans is trying to help me. Is this a service you provide to all humans who have a vampire strangely interested in them, or am I special?" I'm yelling at her. Why am I yelling?

"You're special," she answers.

"I'm a scrawny sixteen-year-old who lives in the projects

of New Orleans. I'm no more special than anyone else in this city."

"You're special to me." What is she talking about? I move through the room, watching the conversation unfold in front of me. Sixteen-year-old Amelia is angry, and Cherie is trying to comfort her.

"I knew your mother. She was a foster child in my home. We grew up together." Cherie and my mother knew each other?

"What? My mother? That can't be. She lived with her grandmother until she died."

"That was a lie. Tammy was put in the foster care system at a very young age. She had a horrible life when she was younger. After she came to my house, she was welcomed and loved." I move toward the couch, staring into my younger eyes. *"She moved in when she was thirteen and I was fifteen. She was the sister I never had, and I loved her like we were blood."*

"What happened?" little me asks.

"By the time she was your age, she was using drugs daily. In the end, the drugs won, and she disappeared." They continue to talk which is drowned out by the realization of my life. My mother was a drug addict who lived as a foster child with a lycan family. This doesn't even feel real.

"I'm not trying to rescue you. I'm trying to help you. I couldn't help your mother, but I can help you." Cherie steps toward the younger me, matching her angry energy. *"I*

don't know why that vampire is after you, but he is, and I refuse to let him have you."

The scene switches. Harrison has me and is taking me to Ophelia's shop. She tries to get me to drink something she created, but I refuse. She asks me to grab a bag from the table on the other side of the room, and when I turn around, she blows something into my face —the same powder as Mr. Sam.

My reality switches back to the small shotgun house, and Mr. Sam standing in front of me. "There she is," he says with a smile.

"Amelia? Are you okay?" Topher's standing over me like a mother hen.

It takes a few minutes to acclimate my mind. "Yes, I'm okay."

"Did you remember anything?"

I slide forward, putting my head in my hands. "I remember everything." I jump to my feet and head straight for the door. "Thank you, Mr. Sam."

"Anytime, young lady. Topher, come back to see me."

I'm on the porch before Topher says his goodbyes. "What the hell, Amelia?"

I run to my SUV and climb inside quickly. Topher jumps in the passenger seat as I floor it, taking us out of the quaint neighborhood and back to the Quarter.

"Are you going to tell me what's going on?"

"I need to see Edon."

"Edon? What does he have to do with all of this?"

"That's exactly what I'm going to find out."

We make it to the other side of the river in record time. I stop in front of the lycan bar where I hope Edon will be in his office. Topher hasn't asked any more questions since we left Algiers, and we run together inside the bar.

"Whatever's bothering you, you need to leave outside of his office. My father has never done anything to harm you. Remember that," Topher announces before we're inside.

I take a deep breath and nod. He opens the door, and Edon stands from his desk. "Topher, Amelia. It's good to see you." He looks between the two of us. "Is everything okay?"

"May I sit?" I point at the empty chair in front of his desk.

"Please."

I sit down, taking a deep breath. "I don't know where to start, so I'm just going to blurt it out."

"Okay?" Edon looks as confused as I feel.

"Why did my mother live with your wife's family?"

Edon wrinkles his forehead. "What?"

"Why did Tammy live with your wife's family? She was a foster child in their home, why?"

He shrugs. "I remember her parents hosting foster children from time to time. I don't remember anyone specific. Your mother was one of the kids?"

"She was."

Edon stares at me as intently as I'm staring at him.

"I don't know what information you think I'm holding. Cherie and I knew each other as kids. We were part of the same pack, and her father was well-known and respected. But we weren't close enough that I would've met the kids in her home." He stands, moving to a bookshelf behind him. "Her family was known to offer wayward kids a home throughout the years."

"That's why Cherie wanted to protect me. She said my mother was lost to drugs, and she couldn't protect her. She wanted to keep me from the same fate."

He crosses his arms in front of his chest. "That sounds like her. She was always trying to save the world."

"Was my mother a lycanthrope?" Edon looks up at my words.

"What?"

"Was she a werewolf?" I repeat.

"I...I don't know," he stutters over his words.

"Dad?" Topher interrupts for the first time. "Is there a possibility that Amelia's mother could be lycan?" Edon doesn't answer.

"Did you know I met Harrison back then when I was in high school?"

Edon looks at the floor. "I did."

"Did you know that he groomed me from childhood to be his...his Penelope? That bastard stalked a teenager, and killed her mother all in the name of me becoming his new pet, his lover? Who the hell knows what his reasons really were."

"Amelia, please sit down." Edon motions toward the now empty chair. "I'll tell you everything I know."

I sit, keeping the scowl on my face. "I did know he was grooming you. That's why we stepped in."

"By we, you mean Cherie?"

"No, we. Cherie was the one who could get to you, and I was the one who could get to Harrison." He sighs. "You're right. Cherie knew your mother. They were friends until Tammy couldn't control her...issues...any longer. She searched for her for years without luck."

"Why Tammy? Why was she so obsessed with keeping her safe?"

Edon sighs loudly. "Ah, dammit. You're asking me to betray my wife by telling you this."

"Your wife's dead, Edon." My words are cruel and harsh. I don't look at Topher. I don't want to know the pain I just caused. "You can do her service by telling me the truth. No one has told me the truth my entire life. Can we please start now?"

Edon sighs before continuing. "Tammy's father was lycan. Her mother was human."

I stare blankly at the Alpha Wolf of New Orleans. "My mother was half-wolf?"

"Is that possible?" Topher asks. "I thought our DNA wasn't compatible."

"It's extremely rare, but yes, it's possible. Only one out of every ten thousand births survive."

"There's been a goddamn scientific study on it?" I stand, stomping my way to the other side of the room.

"What does that make me? Some sort of a vampire-wolf hybrid?"

"Something like that," Edon answers.

"Holy shit," Topher whispers.

"I don't have nor have ever had any characteristics of lycan. I was an average, run-of-the-mill human until I was turned into a vampire."

"Not yet, at least. We don't know what will happen in the heat of the moment."

"You do realize how insane this sounds?" I turn back toward the duo. "Did Harrison know? Does Viktor know?"

"No. The secret was only known by Cherie and me. The amount of lycan blood in your system is so small, it would be nearly untraceable, even for an ancient vampire."

"Did Harrison know Tammy was half-wolf?"

"Probably. He could most likely smell and taste it in her blood."

"Then he sure as hell knew there was wolf blood in me, too." I punch my fist into the wall, knocking a softball-sized hole in the cinder block. How could I have been so stupid?

"That's why he wanted me. It had nothing to do with Penelope. Did he intend on turning me into a vampire the entire time? All in the name of a fucked-up science experiment?"

"Chamberlin's dead. No one except for him could tell you his reasoning, but I'm sure it wasn't anything good."

"Harrison killed Cherie, didn't he?"

Edon looks down. "Not personally, but I'm sure he was involved."

"Dad?" Topher turns on his father. "Was she killed by a vampire?"

He shakes his head. "Wolf."

Topher's entire demeanor changes. "Who was it?" His face begins to transform, taking on wolf features.

"I took care of it," Edon answers. "There were five of them. They're dead."

"May I leave?" Topher asks his father. Edon nods. "Amelia?"

"I'll take over." Edon barely gets the words out before Topher disappears from the room.

"I've told Topher many times, and I'll tell you the same. I don't need a babysitter." I turn, following the young wolf out of the bar.

"Topher!" I yell after him. He doesn't turn back. Why am I calling after him? I don't need him. I don't need anyone. It's always been me against the world. Why should today be any different?

the point of no return

BACK IN THE privacy of my loft, I send a text to Violet. How much of this shit did she know about?

> Did you know?

It doesn't take long for her to respond.

> Is this the beginning of a joke?

> Did you know about me? Know about Tammy?

She's slower responding.

> Yes.

> How could you look me in the face and lie?

I didn't lie. You never asked, and I never shared.

Vampire semantics. You should've told me.

You're right. I should've. I'm sorry.

I don't respond. Instead, I collapse on the couch and feel sorry for myself. I'm not waiting for anyone to rescue me this time. I pull out my kindle and straight back to the book I was working on this morning, opening it to where I stopped earlier. I read one chapter into the fated mate wolf story and close the cover of my device. Nope.

Opening my laptop, I search for any information related to Tammy Lockhart. Just as I've found every other millionth time I've searched, there's not much to find. Information on the body discovered in the Quarter and the eventual identification of the victim is the only information I find. It's as if Tammy Lockhart didn't exist before then.

I switch gears and begin searching for information on Cherie St. James. I don't know her maiden name, but her married name is a good start. Information on her death pulls up immediately.

The mangled body of a woman was discovered near an abandoned home in Algiers, Monday night. Police are reporting that the unidentified woman was missing her

*arms and legs, which were subsequently found in a trash
bag nearby.*

Oh, my God. That's horrible. Edon said her death
was caused by wolves. Why would they cut off her arms
and legs? I search the trenches of Google until I finally
find a mention of a marriage announcement from when
she and Edon were married. Several clicks later, I have
what has to be their marriage certificate on my screen.

*Cherie Elise Mathis married Edon Christopher St. James
on February 14, 1992.*

Armed with her last name, I search for any information on Cherie Mathis and am met with pages stem-
ming from awards days in elementary school to her
high school graduation announcement. One headline
stands out from the rest.

*Young teen accused of murdering her foster father,
William Mathis.*

William Mathis? Are they related? A quick glance
through the article answers the question I already
knew. William and Judy Mathis were the parents of two
children of their own and countless foster children
through the years. William's alleged murderer was a
minor living with the Mathis family for a short period
of time. My heart jumps into my throat, and I know the

answer without asking. Tammy, my mother, killed Cherie's father. Holy shit. Why would my mother kill her foster father? The woman I knew as my mother was a drug addict and a contestant for "World's Worst Mother," but she wasn't a murderer, was she?

I grab my laptop and head down the stairs, straight to Topher's house. It takes several loud bangs before he opens the door.

"Amelia, I don't feel like having company."

"I know, and I'm sorry. I found something you need to see." I hold the laptop in front of my face.

"Can it wait? I'll check in with you tomorrow." He pushes the door, trying to shut out me and the world.

"No, it can't." I stick my foot in the crack, blocking it from closing.

Topher sighs deeply. "Fine." He opens the door wide, and I hurry in before he changes his mind.

He sits on the opposite side of the couch, pulling his long legs up beside him. "What's so important?" I open the laptop, pulling up the pages I found earlier. I skip the article on his mother's death and jump straight to the one about his grandfather, William Mathis. He reads through the article completely. "My grandfather was murdered by one of his foster children?"

"I think my mother was the one who killed him."

"This day just keeps getting better." Topher puts my laptop down before heading to the refrigerator. "I need a beer. Want something to drink?"

"No, I'm good. Thanks." I wait for him to sit back

down before asking the question that's been plaguing me since reading the article. "When a lycanthrope transforms into a wolf for the first time, what happens?"

He shrugs. "Unbelievable pain, confusion, anger, frustration. Should I go on?" He takes a swig of the already nearly empty beer.

"When you wolf out for the first time, do you lose control?"

"I didn't. It was painful, but I don't remember going crazy. None of my brothers did either."

"What about a hybrid? Could a hybrid lose control?"

"Maybe? I didn't even know hybrids were a possibility until today. You think your mother wolfed out for the first time and killed my grandfather during the process?"

"How else would a human teenager kill a full-size lycanthrope man?"

He heads back to the fridge for another drink. "You're assuming that Tammy was the one that killed him. You heard Edon say there were lots of foster children in their home. It could've been any of them that killed him."

"Except it wasn't. I can't explain how I know, but I do." I pull up my search on Tammy Lockhart. "There's no information on her except for her death records. What if that's not her real name?"

"She was a foster kid. Maybe they changed her

name to protect her." Topher grabs his phone. "I have a friend that works in city records. If Lockhart isn't her real name, he should be able to find it." He sends a quick text before collapsing his head on the cushion behind him and closing his eyes. "I'll have to admit. When I agreed to protect you, this wasn't the direction I thought it would take."

"Yeah, I'd say I was sorry, but I don't need protection, anyway."

"So, you keep telling me." He pulls his buzzing phone in front of him. "He says he'll check and get back to me. Depending on how busy he is, it may be a day or two." I gather my laptop and start to head to the door. "You might as well stay. We can watch movie number four from here just as well as we can from your place."

"Are you sure you're up to it?"

"No, but I need the company. I'm not a fan of being alone right now." His voice sounds sad.

"Think you can stay awake this time?"

"Maybe."

He starts movie number four and stops it within the first five minutes. "Have you ever wanted to hunt?"

"Honestly, no. But I did drink human blood once."

"Spill," he says, toasting his beer toward me. "And I mean that in a non-ironic way."

"It was the cult. One of the members slit her throat in front of me. I couldn't resist the bloodlust."

"Slit her own throat? Oh, my God. That's horrible."

"It was. She was dying in front of me, and I drank her blood. I lost control."

Topher doesn't respond, just starts the movie back up. "Think Jacob will come to the wedding?"

"Do you want to know?"

"No. I like living on the edge. No spoilers, please." We watch the rest of the movie in silence. I notice him making faces during the honeymoon scenes, but he stays quiet. He actually looks slightly embarrassed. The end credits roll, and Topher squirms in his seat.

"That was kind of weird."

"You can't say I didn't warn you about the imprinting."

"You did, but it was even weirder to see."

I turn, facing the wolf. "Can I ask you something personal?"

He shrugs. "Sure."

"What do you look like in wolf form?"

Topher smiles. "Like a normal wolf, only larger. Not like the movie versions. I can walk on two legs or four when in wolf form."

"Seriously? A bipedal wolf would be terrifying. What color is your fur?"

He pulls his dark hair away from his scalp. "Same color. What do you look like as a vampire?"

I flash my teeth at him, and he pretends to grimace. "That's it. That's all I can do."

"Impressively non-terrifying."

I flip him off as his phone buzzes. "It's my friend. He

says he had trouble finding it, but finally located information in her foster care folder. Your mother's name was changed. Originally, her last name was O'Connell."

"O'Connell? Why does that name feel familiar? Are there any Irish lycan hanging around the city?"

Topher slides his legs off the couch. "Tyler O'Connell was the Alpha before my dad."

"Did he have a son? Jacob?"

He looks at me like I've lost my mind. "Are you confusing *Twilight* with real life?"

"No, I'm being serious. It's a memory that came back this morning. There was a boy, his name was Jacob O'Connell. He was lycan." I stop, trying to remember the details. "His father was Alpha."

"He did. I remember him, I think. Tyler's been gone a long time, but he would've been too young to be Tammy's father."

"Her brother, maybe?" Topher stands, grabbing what looks like a photo album off of his bookshelves.

"There's a picture of Tyler somewhere in here." I resist the sarcasm that's begging to be let out, knowing that he has a photo album. He flips through the pages, landing on one in particular. He sets the book in front of me. "This is Tyler."

"That's him. I remember his face. Jacob introduced us." I pull the book closer, looking closely at every detail. "They have the same nose, I think. He and my mom. I don't remember too much about her, but his nose looks familiar."

"I don't know who Tyler's father was, but if Tyler was Alpha, chances are his father was important to the pack."

"Who can we ask?"

"Edon is the one with the knowledge. After this afternoon, right now is the best time to contact him."

"Do you know what happened to Jacob? He would've been a little younger than you."

"I think he moved to Atlanta. I remember hearing something about him leaving New Orleans after Tyler died."

I grab a spiral notebook off his coffee table and begin to take notes. Drawing a line down the middle I label one side with "Things we know," and the other with, "Things we don't know."

"When I was working on my doctorate, this would help me get everything organized."

"You have a Ph.D.?"

"Yes. Why do you sound so surprised?"

"Maybe not surprised, just...yeah, surprised. What's it in?"

"Mythological Creatures of Europe."

"You chose well." He laughs.

"Yeah. I was always drawn to mythology. After what we discovered today, it makes sense." I stop writing. "Topher, do you think I could turn into a wolf?"

"I doubt it. Some full-blooded lycan never change. Just because someone has the gene, doesn't automatically mean they'll change."

"So, there are full-blooded lycan that will never wolf out? What happens to them?"

He shrugs. "They go on to live normal, happy, wolfless lives."

I turn my attention back to the notebook. "Okay. Things we know. Tammy O'Connell was my mother's name." I write as I speak.

"She was half-lycan," Topher adds.

"She killed her foster father."

"We don't know that. You need to add a new column for things we are making assumptions about." Topher points to the notebook.

I ignore him and under the "things we don't know column," I add. "Why she did it."

"Why do you think Chamberlin killed Tammy?"

I set my pen down. "Maybe he was finished with her. I don't know. Could have been anything." I stare at the nearly empty paper in front of me. "Shit. We barely know anything."

"It's getting late. Let's call it a night and finish this stupid movie series. We'll do more research tomorrow." He turns Netflix back on and starts the last movie.

"I'm getting a little tired of Bella. Are you sure you want to watch this tonight?"

"No." He pushes play. "But we're committed at this point. We're past the point of no return, and there's no going back."

death and destruction

THE SUN PEERS in through the large windows in Topher's loft. He fell asleep on the couch after the movie, and I didn't try to wake him. My night was spent looking for more information and reading a book I downloaded onto my laptop. I didn't find any information other than what we already know. I look at the giant wolf on the other end of the sectional. Since he showed up in Jamaica, Topher's been at my side, insisting he is my protector. Before him, his mother protected me. What happened in the middle? Was I on my own? Were they watching me from a distance? I scratch my head, trying to clear all the questions away. One mystery at a time, Amelia.

Topher's phone begins to buzz. It stops several seconds later only to start again. I don't know whether to try and answer it or let it keep ringing. My phone starts ringing the second his stops. The number isn't one I recognize.

"Hello?" I answer.

"Amelia?" Edon's voice is on the other end. *"Wake Topher up, please. Something's happened."*

I kick Topher's feet, startling him. "What the hell, Amelia?"

"He's awake." I put Edon on speakerphone. *"He can hear you. What's going on?"*

"There was a hit on a lycan-owned bar last night. It has all the makings of the cult."

"Where?" Topher asks, sitting up.

"The Copper Kettle," Edon answers.

"I know where that is. We're on our way," I answer for the both of us. Topher throws on a pair of jeans and a T-shirt, and we head downstairs to the Quarter. It doesn't take long before we're standing in front of the inconspicuous door.

"This is just like before, hitting small bars that are owned by wolves." We enter the dark room, and the overwhelming smell of blood hits me instantly. My vampire eyes can see the destruction and bodies scattered throughout.

"Something bad happened here," Topher says. "Why don't they have the lights on?" He flips his phone flashlight on, shining it around on the bloody floor. "What the hell?"

"Topher," Edon's deep voice calls across the room. "We're keeping the lights off on purpose." We walk toward his voice and find the reason for the darkness. On the floor huddled in a ball is a young boy. He doesn't look any older than seven or eight. He's crying and shaking uncontrollably. "He won't move, and we don't want to scare him any more than he already is," Edon whispers.

"Is he lycan?" I ask. Edon nods. "Where are his parents?" He nudges his head backward and closes his eyes. I know without asking, they're dead.

I kneel next to the young boy. "Hi. My name is Amelia. Do you mind if I sit next to you?" The boy doesn't respond. Crossing my legs in front of me, I lower myself next to him.

"Home," the boy mutters.

"We're going to take you home. Can you tell me your name?"

"Brayden," he answers, sliding closer to me. He wraps his arms around mine and pulls me close.

"Do you think you can walk, Brayden?"

"Where's my mom?"

I don't dare turn toward the destruction behind me. "I'm not sure right now. Why don't you come outside with me, and my friend Topher will see if he can find her?" Topher waves at the boy.

"Okay," he whispers. He clings on to me, and I pull him to a standing position, keeping his head buried below my arm so he can't see the destruction around him. We walk slowly toward the door and away from the aftermath of insanity. Once outside, the sunlight makes him blink quickly. He's still shaking but has stopped crying. Humans passing by stare but, thankfully, don't stop to ask what's happening.

I don't ask him any more questions. He's clearly been through enough trauma. Asking him to remember details isn't what he needs right now. "Did you know I grew up not far from here?" I point in the direction of the Calliope Apartments. I've always loved the Quarter. I even went to school down here.

"Me, too," he whispers.

"How old are you, Brayden?"

"Seven."

"Do you know how brave you are?" He shakes his head. "You are super brave. What do you like to do for fun?"

"Draw," he answers.

"Really? I've never been very good at drawing. That didn't keep me from trying, though. What's your favorite thing to draw?"

"Brayden?" a middle-aged woman calls, running down the sidewalk. She stops in front of us. "Get your bloodsucking hands off my nephew."

"Aunt Macie?"

"It's me, baby." The woman glares at me, daring me to try anything.

"Brayden was scared. He came outside with me, and we were talking about drawing, weren't we, Bud?" Brayden wraps his arms around his aunt and begins to cry again.

"It's okay, baby. I'm here." She steers him away from the bar and the horrible, bloodsucking vampire that comforted him moments earlier.

I enter the bar, finding the lights on and blood covering nearly every surface. "What the hell happened in here?" I say to no one in particular. The walls, floor, and even the ceiling are covered in blood splatter. It's as if a tornado of destruction swept through.

"Amelia?" Topher calls from across the room. "Come look at this."

He's kneeling over a young woman with what looks like loaded ammo strapped to her chest. "Is she wearing a suicide vest?"

"Looks that way." He turns the girl over. "None of them were detonated." My memory flashes back to Zoe. She wore something exactly like this and held the detonator in her hand.

"Check her hands. But be careful. She may have the detonator button concealed."

He checks both, finding nothing. "If the bombs didn't go off, what could've done this?"

"Can you tell how she died?"

"Her throat's been ripped out."

"Is that something a lycan would've done?"

Topher sits back on his knees and scoffs. "Not a usual means of killing, but anything's possible. When a wolf kills, the injuries aren't as clean."

"If it wasn't a wolf or a bomb, what does that leave?"

"A vampire?" he asks the question already floating around in my mind.

I look around. "If this was a vampire, they're stronger than anyone I know."

"Viktor?"

I shake my head. "No. He wouldn't do something like this. The only person I know capable of this kind of mindless destruction is Hypatia."

"Why would a member of the council destroy lycan? It doesn't make sense."

"Because she's a crazy bitch."

Edon moves in front of us, blocking the light. "What are you thinking?" he asks.

I sigh before answering. "This is the work of a vampire."

He shifts from one foot to the other. "That's what I'm thinking, too. Could Viktor have done this?"

"No. Viktor would never do something like this. Yes, he's capable, but he's not the monster he portrays himself as."

"I know, but I needed to ask." He nudges the girl in front of us. "She's human. With that thing strapped to her chest, there's no question she's a member of the cult."

"Looks like she never was able to become the angel," I remember the rules of the cult and how the angels were chosen to destroy the vile creatures of the city.

"Walk with me," Edon says, moving away from the

girl. Topher and I follow obediently through the door and onto the street. "I did a little digging yesterday."

"And?" I ask impatiently.

"I always knew your mother was half lycan, but never knew who her father was or why Cherie made me swear to protect you." I stare wide-eyed, not sure what he's about to say. "I was able to search through some lycan records last night and think I discovered who he was. Originally, I thought her father was the wolf, but it turns out it was her mother."

"What?" I ask, confused.

"Tammy's father was human, and her mother was a lycanthrope. It was a one-night stand. He never knew anything about Tammy. Her mother gave birth to her, then dumped her into the foster care system."

I stop walking, trying to absorb the information he's telling me.

"Her mother came from an influential lycan family..."

"The O'Connell family," I interrupt.

"Yes, how'd you know that?"

"Topher has a friend in city records."

He sighs. "She stayed in the system until Cherie's father learned about her existence. I don't know how he found out, but he did. He brought her into his house when she was around five. That's all I could find."

"My grandmother was lycan?"

"Yes. From a very powerful line."

"Holy shit," I whisper. "Is she still alive? My grandmother?"

"I don't know. After she dumped your mother, her father shipped her to another pack."

I turn toward Topher. "I know. More research," he speaks before I can. His voice sounding exasperated.

"Will you two come with me to Viktor's?" Every fiber in my soul stops at once.

"I'd rather not if it's all the same to you. Right now, isn't the best time for Viktor and me. He doesn't want to see me, and I'm feeling the same."

"I understand. You also understand why I don't want to leave you alone at the moment?"

I cross my arms across my chest. "No, I don't understand that. I'm a damn vampire. I can take care of myself."

"Can you take care of yourself against something capable of the destruction we just left? If you're that powerful, then you should be protecting me."

"No, I couldn't, but what makes you think the vampire that did that would be after me?"

"Gut feeling," Edon answers.

"Maybe you could wait outside?" Topher adds.

"No. Viktor would know I was there. Waiting outside is cowardly. I'll go."

Edon's car isn't far from the bar, and the three of us climb inside for the drive across the lake. Pulling in front of his house, I'm surprised at how unattached I feel. This seems like a lifetime ago. I feel him the moment we park.

"You okay back there?" Edon asks.

"I'm not sure yet," I answer truthfully.

I follow the two giants to the front door, which opens before we step onto the porch. "Edon, Christopher, Amelia. To what do I owe the pleasure?"

"Something happened last night, and I want your opinion," Edon answers for all of us.

"Of course." He opens the door wide, inviting us inside. I know him well enough to realize he's putting on a show, and it pisses me off. "What's happened?"

"One of our bars was attacked."

"The cult?" Viktor asks.

"The cult was involved, but we don't believe they're the ones who initiated the attack."

Viktor sits back in his chair, crossing his long legs at the knee. Watching him across from me, I'm surprised at what I feel. Instead of the broken-hearted little girl I expected to be dealing with, I feel nothing. When did that happen? His dark hair is smoothed close to the scalp, and he's wearing his signature waistcoat and high-waisted pants. He seems to have stepped back in time and looks like he did when we first met.

"Why don't you tell me the details?"

"There was a young girl with an explosive vest strapped on. But like the rest of the patrons of the bar, she was dead, and the explosives weren't detonated," Topher fills in the blanks. "Her throat was ripped out."

"Sounds like a vampire," Viktor states the obvious. "Not many around here are capable of such destruction."

"You are," I speak for the first time, and for the first time Viktor looks at me.

"You are right, my dear, but I can assure you it wasn't me."

"No one thinks it was you," Edon smooths the water before the ripples begin.

"Then why are you here?"

"There's only one other vampire in the area capable of that kind of destruction. Hypatia," I spew.

On cue, she comes down the staircase, completely naked. "Did I hear my name? What is it you think I've done?" She moves behind Viktor, running her hands seductively over his shoulders. "Hello, Alicia. How have you been?"

"I'm great, thanks." I don't bother to correct her. I stand, heading toward the door. Edon and Topher are right on my heels without question.

"I'll be in touch," Edon says, closing the door behind us.

It's not until we're halfway across the lake that Topher speaks, interrupting the silence. "What the hell was that?"

"That, my friend, was Hypatia, in all of her glory."

"Why do I feel dirty now? She gave me the creeps."

"Same," I answer.

a vampire who won't kill a fish

EDON DROPS me off at my loft, and not to my surprise, Topher exits the car behind me. "Where are you going?"

"With you."

I sigh louder than normal. "Topher. How many times…"

"I know. You don't need a babysitter." He changes his voice to match the timbre of mine, and I resist the urge to bitch slap him.

"I'll just sit here on the curb." He looks around at the crowded street. "Although, being on Bourbon Street, I'll either be propositioned or kidnapped or both within the next few minutes." He sits on the curb, bringing his long knees to his chin. He's right. A group of young girls have already spotted him and are working their way toward him.

"Come on." He jumps up and follows me inside.

"Are you okay? I mean, after seeing Viktor."

I plop on the couch before answering. "Surprisingly, I am. I don't know why, but I am. Seeing him didn't affect me the way I thought it would."

"Maybe you never really loved him."

I scoff. "One thing I've learned is that I have severe daddy issues. The last two men I've slept with were older and not what I needed."

"What do you need?"

I stand, heading toward the refrigerator. "If I knew that, I wouldn't be here with you, my friend."

Topher stands. "Do you mind if I use your shower? I feel gross after being inside that bar."

"Sure. Make yourself at home. You're not going to leave anyway." He laughs, heading into the bathroom. I barely have time to drag my laptop out before he reappears in the doorway. He's shirtless and the towel wrapped around his waist is hanging on for dear life. I clear my throat awkwardly. "Why are you naked in my doorframe?"

"You told me to make myself at home."

"That didn't include standing nearly naked in my living room." Topher winks before turning to go back into the bathroom. What the hell was that? "Did you just wink at me?"

"There was something in my eye." I can hear the amusement in his voice.

"You're getting on my nerves."

"Am I, though?"

"Yes!" I yell as the door closes behind him. He's really not on my nerves, but I'm not going to share that. The fact is, I enjoy the distraction and company. Although, wild horses couldn't drag that information out of me. My doorbell rings below, making me jump.

"Was that the doorbell?"

"It was. Maybe someone saw your nearly naked show from the street and wants to come in for a closer view."

"In that case, let them in."

I laugh, opening the door to the spiral staircase. A familiar energy punches me in the stomach. I move with vampire speed to the door and open it. The person on the other side isn't who I expect to see. A young woman with bright red hair smiles widely as I look past her, looking for my tiny maker.

"Amelia?" her soft voice calls my name.

For the first time, I look into the eyes of the girl at my door. "Celeste?"

She smiles a familiar smile before wrapping her arms around my shoulders and pulling me tight. I pull away, not sure how to feel. "It's me," she says with a smile.

"Oh, my God. Celeste? You're...you're all grown up."

"I am."

"I'm speechless." I stare at the beautiful young woman standing in front of me. "I'm sorry. Please come in." I step to the side, giving her room to enter. She's at least a foot taller than me, and her legs are nearly as long as my entire torso and legs combined.

"This is beautiful," she says, following me upstairs and entering into the loft.

"Have you been to see your father yet?"

"No. I came here first."

"How did you find me? I thought our connection was lost."

She laughs softly. "After the transformation was complete, I was able to feel you again. Not as strong, but there, nonetheless."

Topher walks back into the room, thankfully, fully dressed. "Amelia?"

"Topher, this is Celeste. My maker." She smiles warmly at the lycanthrope.

"It's a pleasure to meet you, Topher. I'm Celeste."

"So, I gather," he answers, looking between the two of us. "I'd swear if I wasn't sitting here in the same room with both of you, I'd think you were the same person."

"Except for the height difference, of course." I laugh. "Maybe I need to do what you did. Then I wouldn't be mistaken for a teenager any longer."

Celeste sits on the couch. "Tell me everything I've missed."

Topher and I share a look. "I moved out of the Mandeville house and came here. Somehow in the process, I've picked up a wolf babysitter that refuses to leave me alone and enjoys watching *Twilight* movies."

"Enjoy is a strong word. Tolerates is more appropriate," Topher adds.

"I can't get over how beautiful you are." I stare at my maker. Bright blue eyes glisten in the sunlight streaming through the windows. "What happened? How...how did you do this?"

Celeste looks down at her hands. "It's a solution that didn't come without sacrifice."

"What does that mean?"

"Nothing." She smiles. "I need to go visit Daddy. He's going to be pissed when he finds out I came to see you first."

"Don't tell him. There's something you need to know before going to that house."

"What?"

"There's another vampire there. A very ancient vampire." Celeste stares at me patiently. "Hypatia is there with him."

"Hypatia? His maker?"

"Yes."

"Why is she here?"

"Looking for you," Topher answers.

"For me? Why?"

"She's on the council. She's here looking for the immortal child."

Celeste stands. "Well, she won't find one. I'm a grown woman. I have nothing to worry about."

"Hypatia isn't going to care about semantics. She's only going to care that you were once an immortal child. We think she was responsible for killing everyone inside a lycan bar last night."

"Is it the cult?" she asks.

"We don't think they're connected," Topher answers.

"I'll have to say, I've missed you, but I haven't missed the drama of the city." Celeste stands, heading toward the door. "I'll be in touch. For now, I need to go to him." She turns, giving me a warm hug that feels like home.

"I'm glad you're back."

"Me, too." I walk her to the door. "I'll contact you." She gives me another hug before disappearing into the crowd.

"That's the immortal child?" Topher asks.

"That's her. Although, she's not a child any longer." I sit back on the couch. "I'm not sure how Viktor's going to handle her being grown. His entire life has revolved around protecting her. That's the only reason he let Hypatia parade around and hang all over him today. Hypatia's just too dumb to realize it."

"That bothered you, didn't it?"

I slide back on the couch. "No. I think I expected to see her there. He'd do anything to protect Celeste. Sleeping with the enemy isn't out of reach."

He sits next to me, his leg touching mine. "Get that laptop. Let's do some research. After what Edon said, I'm invested in your heritage."

I grab my laptop and the spiral notebook I stole

from his loft. I add "mother was lycan," under the things we know side. Topher opens my laptop and heads straight to Google. "Search for Tammy O'Connell. See if anything pulls up."

"Already on it." He types and searches for a while until he announces he's found absolutely nothing.

"There has to be something."

"The only way we discovered the name O'Connell was through my friend in city records. Those are sealed from public searches." He closes the laptop.

"Wait, search for Jacob O'Connell."

He types a few more words into Google and finds the answer quickly. "Jacob O'Connell is living in Atlanta with his wife and newborn baby." He shows me Jacob's Facebook profile.

"He looks the same as I remember."

"Want me to message him?" he asks.

"And say what, exactly? Hey, Jacob. We haven't talked since your dad was killed trying to protect me, but do you have a great-aunt?"

Topher shrugs. "That works." He starts typing.

"Topher, don't you dare send that."

He laughs. "I'm going to ask him how he's been since we haven't seen each other since we were teenagers. I'm not going to say anything about you."

"Done," he announces, closing the laptop for the second time. "Now what do we do? We're out of *Twilight* movies."

"Ever watched *Harry Potter*?"

He turns toward me with wide eyes. "No, I wasn't allowed to."

"Why?"

"Because of the magic."

I lean my weight into him. "You hold a mythological gene in your blood and turn into a wolf, yet you're not allowed to watch *Harry Potter* because of the *magic* in the story?"

"Sounds about right."

"I have a better idea. It's barely noon. Let's get out of the apartment and go on a hike or something." I stand, propping my hands on my hips.

"A hike? As in outside?"

"As in outside."

"I get itchy," Topher whines, making me laugh.

"You are the wimpiest wolf I've ever met."

He jumps to his feet. "I'm only kidding. Let's go on a hike. You might want to bring some sunscreen and a big hat. I'd hate for you to sparkle in public."

I playfully slap his thigh. "I told you that's a myth. I don't sparkle."

"I'll be the judge of that."

......

Topher drives my BMW across the river toward the marshlands. All four windows are down, and he's blaring Coldplay through the speakers. Anyone within fifty feet has the pleasure of sharing the music with us.

My hair has grown enough that I was able to pull it into a high ponytail. I can only imagine the look my red curls have taken on. I most likely resemble a deranged clown.

Traffic has slowed enough that we're the only ones on the dirt road. "Do you know where we're going?" I yell over the music.

"What?"

I turn down Coldplay and ask the question again. "Yes!" he screams, turning the volume to full blast. A few minutes later he pulls into the driveway of a house on pillars. The driveway reminds me of the famous scene from *Gone with the Wind*. Ancient live oak trees line the driveway, each full of Spanish moss. Pulling underneath the house, he parks the car. Sounds of locusts and frogs fill my ears as soon as the music stops.

"This is beautiful. Are we trespassing?"

"Maybe." He smiles.

I follow him to the marsh behind the house. For the first time in a while, I can breathe. Fresh air fills my lungs. "Topher, this is perfect. I don't care if we are trespassing."

"Come on." He grabs my hand, pulling me up the stairs to a wraparound porch. He slides a flower pot over, revealing a key hidden beneath.

"Are we breaking and entering now?"

"Maybe," he repeats.

We enter the home, and I'm drawn to the photographs covering the far wall. Pictures of Edon and

Cherie stare back at me. Topher varies in age in each picture. "Is this your awkward stage?"

"Rude. Like you never had an awkward stage."

"My entire life has been an awkward stage."

"I think you're beautiful," he says, making me feel even more awkward.

"We need to get your eyes checked." I laugh off his comment.

"Want to go fishing?"

"Sure? I've never fished before, so you'll have to teach me."

"That, I can do." He takes me back downstairs, and we dig through the locked closet in the carport, finding bait, tackle, and poles.

A few minutes later, we're sitting on the end of a dock with two cane poles in the water. "This feels like a Hallmark movie."

"Is that channel full of movies with wolves and vampires fishing?"

I laugh so loud it echoes off of something in the distance. "It's so quiet out here. I love the Quarter, but if this was mine, I'd never go into town."

"This is where I come when I need to change."

"Change?"

"You know, wolf out. The city isn't the best place for that. You get lots of stares."

"I can imagine. Although, during Mardi Gras, no one would notice."

It's Topher's turn to laugh. "You have a point."

Something tugs on my pole. "Topher, I think I have something."

"Pull the pole quickly, then pull it up slowly. You don't want it to get away."

I follow directions, pulling up a large fish with whiskers. "What is that?"

"It's a catfish." I flop it on the dock next to us and watch as it gasps for air. "We can cook it for dinner."

"It's dying."

"That makes it easier to cook." Topher kneels next to the large fish.

"I don't want it to die."

He looks me in the eyes and smiles. "We won't let it die." He quickly unhooks it and throws it back into the water. "Be free little catfish. Go make lots of babies."

"Thank you," I whisper. "I realize how ironic it is for a vampire to be upset about killing a fish."

"Not ironic at all. Are you done fishing?"

I nod. "Can we just sit here and enjoy the quiet?"

We sit side-by-side, legs touching, and stare into the marsh. "I'm guessing that means you don't want me to talk," he whispers, nudging my leg with his.

"Shh." Topher is different from any man I've been around. Admittedly, that's not many, but his energy is different. It's easy and comfortable—I like it.

the marsh

IT TURNS out the marsh was just what I needed. Topher talks me into staying the night; however, it wasn't difficult. While he sleeps, I've been bouncing back and forth between enjoying the fireflies at the marsh and studying each of the photographs in the house. The walls are full of family photos and seeing them somehow brings the comfort of a family to my lonely soul. Photos must be something Cherie did, and it makes sense why Topher would have a photo album in his loft. I take an old album from a bookshelf and head to the porch to watch the sun peak over the horizon.

I flip through the album, enjoying the pictures of little Topher and his brothers. There are pictures of them at the beach, the mountains, and even at Disney. I laugh at the image of a family of lycan walking around Disney World. The pictures get older the further back I turn. This seems to be an album from Cherie's childhood. One picture grabs my attention immediately. Cherie looks to be around fifteen or sixteen. In the picture are three other children. One of them I recognize immediately—Tammy.

Her hair hangs down her back, and she's wearing shorts and a tank top. She looks around thirteen or maybe a little younger. Tammy is smiling and looks joyful. Not the picture of a future drug addict. The back of the photo has all the kids' names listed. At the bottom is written, Tammy Sue.

"Tammy Sue?" I say out loud to no one. I flip through the rest of the album, not finding any more pictures of her. Returning the album to the shelf I see one that looks even older. As soon as I grab it, a folded piece of paper falls out and to the floor. Opening it, I realize it's a birth certificate for Tammy Sue O'Connell and my heart stops.

"Topher?" I yell into the bedroom.

He's at my side within seconds. "What's this?"

"I...I think it's my mother's birth certificate."

"You were right." He slides the paper from my hand, reading aloud. "Her mother is listed as Judith O'Connell and her father..." He stops before reading the words aloud. "Unidentified."

"That means she didn't want anyone to know who my grandfather was."

Topher is sitting at my laptop before I finish my statement. "According to this, Judith O'Connell is still alive and lives in Biloxi, Mississippi. It looks like she's changed her name to Judith Smith, but luckily Google still has her as both. We could be there in two hours, less if I drive."

Thirty minutes later, we're in my SUV heading to the possible home of my grandmother. "What if the address we found isn't accurate? What if she doesn't like me?"

"How could she not love you? You're her grand-daughter."

"She's a lycanthrope that gave her half-wolf baby up for adoption and changed her name. Maybe she doesn't want to be found."

"If she wanted to hide completely, she should've been more creative with the name change. Something tells me she's going to be happy to see you."

With Topher driving, we pull in front of the beach house in an hour and a half. The house sits directly across from the Gulf of Mexico, overlooking the murky water below. "I'm nervous," I whisper.

"Do you want me to stay in the car?"

I shake my head. "No, I want you to come with me... please."

The perfectly manicured yard is host to flowers of all colors and hues. I take a deep breath and ring the doorbell. A middle-aged woman answers the door. "Can I help you?"

"I'm looking for Judith Smith."

The woman smiles. "That's my mother-in-law." I stare at the woman in front of me. Is she, my aunt?

"My name is Christopher St. James. My friend has been looking for information on her mother. Our search led us here."

"You're lycan, and you're a vampire. What would you possibly want with Judy? There's nothing she can tell you about your mother."

"With all due respect, I think there is. My mother was Tammy Sue O'Connell."

"Tammy?" an elderly voice rings through the door. An older white-haired woman moves beside the younger one, pulling the door open wide enough to see us. "Did you say, Tammy Sue?"

"Yes, ma'am. She was my mother."

"For heaven's sake, Bridget. Move out of the way." The younger woman doesn't look happy as she steps out of the doorway as Judy takes her place. "What do you want?"

"I...I think you're my grandmother."

"Come, sit down." We follow her inside to a sitting room, overlooking the Gulf. Topher sits so close, our legs touch. No doubt he's on edge. "Would you care for anything to eat or drink?" she asks, standing behind her chair.

"No, thank you." I pull the birth certificate out of my bag and hand it to her. "This is my mother's birth certificate. You're listed as her mother."

"Where in the world did you find this? I thought they were all destroyed."

"It's not important," I answer. My voice sounds harsher than intended.

"I guess you're right." She folds the paper and hands it back to me. "Tammy Sue was my child, but she was a freak of nature." I stare at the woman in front of me, not sure how or if to respond. "She was half lycan and half human. Children like that don't survive. If they do, they don't live past childhood, let alone long enough to have their own children."

I don't know why, but this woman is pissing me off. "That child was my mother."

"I can see that," Judy answers. "And you're a bloodsucker." I feel the instant Topher changes into full protection mode. "If you came here thinking there would be some great reconciliation and me welcoming you into my home, you have another thing coming. I never wanted Tammy. I never cared what happened to her, and I certainly don't want anything to do with a bloodsucker who's here after my money."

I stand with Topher at my side. "I am certainly not here for your money. I don't need your money."

"Then why are you here?"

Truthfully, I don't know why I'm here. "I thought maybe we could get to know each other."

Judy laughs. "You thought we could be what? Family?" She slides to the front of her seat. "My brother is dead. Killed by a bloodsucker that I smell on you. If you're here to kill me, then good luck."

For the first time since this whole shit show started, I witness a lycan change into a wolf. The woman stands and transforms instantly into a solid white wolf. She's beautiful in a terrifying way. She snarls, scrapping her nails across the chair she once sat in.

Topher steps in front of me. He's not in wolf form, but his features have changed, telling me he could switch at any time. "If you intend on harming Amelia, I will kill you. I'm younger, stronger, and more powerful. I will keep her safe at any cost. Am I making myself clear?"

The white wolf snarls, slinging slobber across the room. She looks my protector in the eyes before backing down and sitting. She bows her head and closes her eyes. "Leave now," the younger woman says from behind us.

Topher grabs my hand, pulling me to the door and our awaiting car. "What the hell was that?" I ask, once inside the safety of the SUV. "Did my grandmother just try to kill me?"

"She did." Topher hits the gas, and we leave the only blood relative I have behind. "She wasn't in her right mind."

"She seemed like she was fully aware of her actions."

"She's confused. I could tell. Lycanthrope are connected. Sort of a pack thing. Even though we're not from the same pack I could feel inside her mind. She wasn't all there. Don't take the way she acted back there personally."

"How am I not supposed to take that personally? My grandmother wanted to rip me to shreds."

"I'm sorry, Amelia. I wish I knew how to make you feel better, but I don't. Family isn't everything."

"That's easy for you to say. You've been surrounded by family since birth." My one-woman pity party sounds whiny, even to me. "I'm sorry. That's not fair." Topher doesn't respond as we work our way back to New Orleans.

"Amelia, I know you think I grew up in a perfect family straight out of a fairytale, but I didn't. Yes, I had a mother and a father in the house with me most of the time, but it wasn't as perfect as you think it was.

"Edon wasn't Alpha yet but was next in line after Tyler. Which meant he was barely home, and when he was home, there was so much turmoil in the lycan community that he would bring those frustrations with him. I know compared to how you grew up my life looks like the perfect situation, but it wasn't always like that. I've gone months without speaking to Edon and even longer without speaking to any of my brothers." I turn toward my protector. "I'm not trying to say my pain is anything like yours, but not everything's as perfect as it seems."

A single tear streams down his cheek, and for the first time, I see Topher for who he truly is. Someone who's been broken as badly as me. I reach over, take his hand into mine, and squeeze. He wraps his long fingers around mine and squeezes back.

"Not to change the subject or anything, but I wonder how Celeste's and Viktor's reunion went," I change the subject.

"Hopefully, Hypatia was wearing clothes when she got there."

"I'm going to guess she wasn't in the house. At least, I hope she wasn't. Where are we going?" I ask as he drives past the downtown exits.

"Back to the marsh. I don't want to go back to reality just yet."

"That's what I was hoping you'd say." Not long after, we pull back into the moss-covered drive and park underneath the raised house. As soon as the car is shifted into park, I run to the dock and sit at the end. Topher joins me a few minutes later. "What took you so long?"

"I thought it might be a good idea to turn the car off." He laughs.

"I love it here. I think I'm going to buy a house next door one day."

"Or you could just stay here with me."

I turn toward my protector. "What are you saying, Topher?"

He shrugs, laughing off his words. "If I'm going to protect you, it'd be easier if you were nearby."

"I told you…"

"I know," he interrupts, rolling his eyes. He slaps his arm, squishing a mosquito. "Damn, bloodsucker." As soon as the words leave his mouth, he turns toward me, wide-eyed. "Oh, Amelia, I didn't mean anything by that."

I laugh out loud. "I hope you're not putting me and a mosquito in the same category. I can promise, it would be much more than a pinch if I bit you. You didn't offend me, puppy."

"Puppy? I'll have you know I'm the future Alpha of New Orleans along with the duties of such."

"Duties? What kind of duties besides protecting people and keeping the peace are involved?"

"You know. Have lots of wolf babies and help multiply the pack."

Wolf babies? "Is there a future Mrs. Alpha in your line of sight?"

"Are you asking me if I have a girlfriend?" He laughs. "No, I'm single and ready to mingle, if you know what I mean."

I cover my ears with my hands. "I'm too young to hear that."

"Too young? You're close to my age."

"Yeah, but I won't always be. You're going to be an old white wolf like my grandmother, and I'll look the same as I do now."

"I guess I've never thought about that. You get to live forever." He lays back on the dock, sliding his hands behind his head. Muscles in his arms tighten, defining the ridges and tattoos.

"I'm not convinced that's a good thing. A lifetime of loneliness doesn't sound overly exciting."

"You've got Celeste and me."

I laugh. "You're going to be too busy raising wolf babies and running the city of New Orleans. I'll have to find a new protector."

"I thought you don't need a protector?"

"Hypothetically," I answer. "You know, you don't have to honor the oath to protect me. My own grandmother doesn't want to protect me. You aren't responsible for my safety."

He slides his hand to his ear. "What? I can't hear you over the sound of the crickets." He grabs my shoulders, pulling me down beside him. My head rests in the crook of his shoulder. Neither of us tries to move.

"To be honest, I'd be okay with staying just like this, forever." His head lowers, resting on top of mine.

"Me, too."

vampire-napped... again

WE STOP by Topher's loft long enough for him to grab a few changes of clothes before heading back to mine. I don't know when I became okay with him being around constantly, but I am. I've gone through two bottles of goat blood since being back, and honestly, I'm craving a third. I didn't realize how hungry I was.

"You, okay?" Topher asks, standing half-naked in my kitchen. Water drips off the ends of his hair, and the towel is again barely hanging on.

"Yeah, just really hungry."

"Do you need me to sacrifice a goat for you?"

"Ha-ha. Funny. No, I feel better now."

"We need to check in with Edon and find out what, if anything's happened with the cult and the bar from the other night."

"Sounds like a plan. I'm going to take a quick shower. Did you leave me any hot water?"

"No." He laughs as I head into the bathroom. True to his word, the water turns cold halfway through my shower and a slew of curse words echo through my mind as I finish in ice-cold water.

Bourbon Street is especially busy tonight. The two of us get quite a few glances as we walk toward the lycan bar on the north side of the Quarter. "Oh, my God!" a woman screams from the other side of the street. "You're hot!" She runs across the blocked-off street, heading straight toward Topher. It's obvious she's had too much to drink by the amount of staggering she's doing just to get across the street.

Topher holds his hands up, attempting to block the tackle of the woman without much luck. She hits him with the grace of a linebacker, pushing him up against the building behind us. "Excuse me, ma'am. I'm not interested in being accosted." He attempts to push her away without much luck.

"Come with us now, or he dies," a deep voice says from behind. I turn, ready to attack whoever has their hands on me, and meet the faces of two unfamiliar vampires. A man and a woman stand side by side, each baring their teeth in public.

"Who are you?"

"Who we are isn't important. We won't ask again. The lycanthrope will die if you try to fight." I glance back at Topher. A second woman has joined the first, and the two of them have Topher's body hidden from view. "Don't call to him," the woman warns from behind.

In an instant, I'm jerked off the street and away from the crowds. A blindfold is slid over my eyes, and silver bands are wrapped around my wrists. "You made a wise decision," the woman says.

"Who are you?" I spew.

"Didn't we already have this discussion? Who we are isn't important. Who you are is." I have no idea where I'm being taken. The street noise has disappeared and is replaced with the sound of my heart pounding in my chest. I'm shoved into a car and driven somewhere out of the city. With a mask over your eyes, it's crazy how fast you lose track of time and space.

Sometime later, the car stops, and I'm dragged outside. I smell salt in the air. Am I near the Gulf? "Take her inside," the man demands as I'm dragged up a few stairs and inside a building.

Someone throws me into a chair, keeping my hands tied behind my back. "Pull the blindfold off," a new woman's voice says. The cover is ripped from my face, and a familiar vampire sits in the chair across from me. "Hello, Andrea."

"Seriously?" One glance around the room lets me know I'm at Viktor's home in Mandeville, in his private office. "What's the meaning of this? Where's Viktor?"

"I hoped you might know." Hypatia sits in the desk chair, propping her feet on the priceless piece of furniture. "It seems he's missing."

"After the way you came down the stairs last time I was here, can you blame him?"

"Jealous much?"

"Of you? No."

She stands, moving in front of me. "What do you know of his immortal child?"

"Nothing more than the first time we talked. You could've just texted me these questions. Kidnapping me off a busy downtown street wasn't necessary."

"It was very necessary. That yummy wolf you were with will have no doubt headed straight to his daddy-dearest and be telling him all about the bad vampires that nabbed you from his grips." She leans on the desk behind her, and I'm grateful she's wearing clothes.

"Why involve the lycan?"

Hypatia shrugs. "The city is out of control anyway. Why not throw a little turmoil into the mix?"

"You lost Viktor, huh?"

"Not lost, so much as misplaced. Your little farce of a break-up is just meant to throw the council off track. Where is he?"

I stare at the idiot in front of me. "Are you dumb?"

Hypatia changes from the beautiful dark-haired persona she portrays to an ancient gargoyle-looking creature. "How dare you speak to me like that?" her words spew from her mouth. "I have been more than patient with you. I can kill you and this entire town with the snap of my fingers. Is that what you want?"

She's moved so close to my face that she spits on me as she speaks.

"Okay, Thanos." I refuse to let her know how terrified I am inside. No doubt, she can sense it, but I won't let it show.

Hypatia laughs. "*Thanatos* and I go way back." She moves back behind the desk. "Tell Viktor his three months have shortened. He has two weeks to bring the girl to me or you, the girl, and Viktor will all die." She sits back in the chair. "Who knows, I might just kill that little wolf for the fun of it. Of course, I'll have to fuck him first."

Anger fills me with her words. "Bitch," I whisper.

"I may be a bitch, but this bitch is in control of your future. Two weeks," she reminds me. "Take her." Two men appear from nowhere and cover my head with something that smells like shit. "Don't fight them, or it will shorten to one week."

Dammit! The drive across the lake is dreadfully long. "You can take this cover off of my head. I know where I am and what you two look like."

"Shut up," a voice comes from the front. Not long after, the car comes to a stop, and my door is opened. Arms reach in, pulling me from the seat and throwing me on the concrete before the sound of tires screeching on the street is heard.

"What the hell? Amelia?" a deep voice says above me. The shit hood is pulled off, and I see Edon kneeling next to me. At the sight of his face, tears fill my eyes. "What happened?" he pulls me up, gently unwrapping the silver ties from around my wrists.

"Topher?" I say between sobs.

"Inside." He lifts me into his arms, carrying me inside the bar.

"Oh, my God. Amelia?" Topher takes me from his father, carrying me into the office that has once again become my rescue space. He sits down, holding me in his arms. "I'm so sorry. I let you down."

"This wasn't your fault. It was Hypatia. You didn't stand a chance."

Topher pulls me close. "I should've stopped them. I was stupid and let my guard down."

I pull away from his grip. "Stop. You're not the one to blame. Neither of us are." He nods. "Viktor and Celeste are missing."

"What do you mean *missing*?" Edon steps forward.

"Hypatia thought I'd know where he is. She lowered his three-month timeline to two weeks."

"What happens at the end of two weeks?"

"She's going to kill Celeste, Viktor, and me." I leave out her threats toward Topher.

"Did she know about Celeste's...change?" Topher asks.

"I don't think so. She's so arrogant, she would have mentioned it."

I pull my phone from my pocket. The screen is shattered from hitting the concrete. I'm able to see well enough to find Viktor in my contacts. His phone doesn't even ring. Just goes straight to a dial tone. "God, I can't even warn him."

"Where would he go?" Topher asks.

"Anywhere," I whisper. "He has the resources to hide for an eternity if he wants."

"Can you call Celeste?"

I shake my head. "No, she's called me from burner numbers each time I've talked to her. I can't contact either of them."

"Then our problem is solved." Topher runs a hand through his scattered hair.

"Amelia is still in danger. Someone will have to pay for Viktor's crimes. Hypatia will make sure of it." Edon moves closer. "We can hide you, but against someone as strong as Hypatia, we won't be able to keep you hidden long."

"I don't expect you to hide me." I slide off Topher's lap and stand next to his father. "Cherie died because of me. I won't allow either of you or anyone in the pack to die to protect me. I'm not that important."

Topher stands, towering over me. "You have no idea how important you are, do you? You are the product of a lycan hybrid, and you're a vampire. You hold the power of both in your blood. That makes you the most important person in both of our worlds."

"Is that why you're protecting me? It has nothing to do with your mother and an oath to her, it's because of what I am." Dammit, if I didn't think I'd get kidnapped, I'd storm out. "You're no better than Harrison."

"Cherie died protecting you. She did it because of an oath she took to your mother." Edon sounds angry. "Yes, she knew your mother was a hybrid as did the entire pack. When Cherie's father discovered there was a surviving hybrid and she was dumped in the city, he brought her into his home, making her one of his own. He loved her. They all loved her." He sits behind his desk. "He died because of that love."

"Tammy killed him, didn't she?" He doesn't answer. "Didn't she?" I yell.

"Yes. She killed him when she transformed for the first time." He sighs. "With no hybrids surviving before her, no one knew if she would have the ability to turn. Most young wolves turn for the first time around the same time they go through puberty. Most have turned by the time they're thirteen or fourteen." He stands, moving to the other side of the room. "She was sixteen, and everyone assumed she wasn't going to be able to turn."

"Except she did," I whisper.

"Except she did," he confirms. "She was stronger than he expected. Hell, she was stronger than him. He tried to hold her down, protect her from the thrashing as her bones were breaking in half, but she overpowered him, killing him in the process."

"That's why she ran."

Edon nods. "Cherie searched for years, with no luck until she found you."

"Tammy seems to have a knack for leaving people." I fight the tears threatening to fall.

"She fell in with Harrison until he eventually killed her."

"Edon, do you think I can change?"

He sighs before answering. "The amount of lycan blood in you is far outnumbered by the vampire blood. I don't think you can. Plus, you're not a teenager. If you were going to change, it would've happened by now."

"What if I can?"

"Then you'd be the most powerful creature of all of us with the ability to unite lycan and vampire together."

Topher wraps his long arm around my shoulders. "Come on, let's get you home."

"Topher," Edon warns.

"I've got her. I won't let anything happen to her."

Edon nods. "I'll send extra patrols outside."

"We're going to my loft." I allow Topher to guide me out of the bar. Once on the street, I pull away, not wanting to appear weak.

We walk in silence, and Topher watches each person as they pass, assessing them for threats. It doesn't take long before we're safely inside with all doors locked, and the blinds pulled. "Amelia, I'm sorry."

I move in front of him. "Stop apologizing. It's not your fault."

"It is my fault! I let you down."

I push his shoulders, shoving him back into the brick wall. "Stop dammit. I'm fine. Hypatia was just trying to make a point. She made it. I'm fine. Let's go on with life."

Topher stares into my eyes. The tension between us is palpable, and I can't pull my eyes away from his. His eyes turn down to my mouth, and the tension ramps up a notch. I don't wait for him to make the first move. Instead, I close the gap between us, putting my lips on his. Topher doesn't hesitate. Strong arms wrap around my waist, lifting me onto his chest. I wrap my legs around his back, latching them tightly around his ass. One kiss has turned into a kissing frenzy, and I can't get enough of him. He carries me into the bedroom, lowering me onto the bed.

He strips off his shirt, giving me full view of the abs I've tried not to stare at. Lowering his weight on top of me, I feel his entire erection. An embarrassingly loud sigh leaves my lips as it pushes against my body.

What are you doing, Amelia? Yes, you want this, but you're doing exactly what you've done two times before. "Stop." I push his chest away from me. "I can't do this."

Topher pulls away with a confused look on his face. "Did I misread the energy between us?"

"No, the energy is strong, and I really want to do this, but I need to stop falling into bed with every creature that comes my way."

"Is that what I am to you? A creature?"

"No, you're my friend."

Topher stands, moving away from the bed. "I'll be in the shower."

"Topher?" He keeps moving, closing the door behind him.

another attack

THE TENSION in the loft is palpable. Topher hasn't said two words to me since "the incident," and I keep finding myself staring at his package. My stomach rumbles from hunger. Why am I so hungry? I usually drink one bottle of blood every few days. I've had two already today and heading to the refrigerator for number three.

"Want a beer?" I ask, staring into the metal ice box.

"No," is all he says.

I grab two red bottles and finish one before I return to the couch. As soon as I sit down, Topher stands, moving toward the bedroom. "Topher. We need to talk about this."

"There's nothing to talk about. Besides, I'm a creature. Creatures don't talk."

"Are you seriously going to act like that?"

He turns. "Like what? A creature?"

"You're being an asshole."

"Am I? Maybe I need to find a group where I can discuss my issues. *Asshole Creatures Anonymous*?"

I can't control the laughter his words bring. "Is that a thing?"

He crosses his arms in front of his chest and tries to hold in a smile. "Maybe."

"I get that you don't want to talk, but can I at least explain?" I move toward him, finishing off the second red bottle.

"I'm still standing here."

I lean against the wall in front of him. "I cannot tell you just how attracted I am to you. Damn, have you seen yourself in the mirror? You're hot. You're sweet, and you're kind...a triple threat. I want nothing more than to jump your bones and fuck your brains out."

"I'm okay with that."

"Don't get me wrong, I do plan on exploring every inch of you and then some, but not now. Not until my life becomes my own. I've spent my entire life being a victim. A child who was abandoned by her drugged-out mother and left to live life on her own. A victim of a psychopathic vampire who stalked me from childhood and nearly killed me." I look down before continuing. "And Viktor. He didn't try to hurt me, but he scared the shit out of me when we first met, and I still flocked to him like a little lost puppy. Now there's an ancient vampire hell-bent on killing me because of who my maker is. It's time for me to become what and who I'm meant to be, and I need to do it for me, not for someone else."

Topher's eyes soften. "I would never expect you to do anything for me, but I understand."

"Thank you." I reach out, touching his arm.

"Can we sit and cuddle a little bit?"

"I'd like that." I lead him to the couch and hand him the remote. "It's *Harry Potter* time. I won't tell Edon."

Topher laughs, turning on the first movie. I curl up next to him, and he wraps his long arms easily around my body. His arms are warm and comfortable. I lace my fingers through his, pulling them close to my chest. Outside, the sky turns dark as large raindrops hit the window, echoing through the loft.

Halfway through the first movie, my stomach rumbles again. "Want me to get you another drink?"

"I already had two. That makes four today. I don't know why I'm so hungry."

"Maybe you're growing?" He says with a laugh.

"Wouldn't that be nice? I'd love to grow a foot, hell, I'd settle with six inches." I turn, facing him. "I drank the last blood earlier. I'll be fine."

I settle back into Topher's arms as he starts movie number two. Not long after the opening credits roll, a loud explosion rattles the entire building. Both of us are on our feet in an instant. "What was that?"

"It sounded like something blew up." We stare out the windows as people run past on the street below.

"We need to check it out," I say, running toward the door.

"Amelia, we need to stay put. You're safest inside this loft, with me."

"Topher, if it was an explosion, it's the cult. We need to find out."

He sighs loudly. "Promise me you won't do anything dumb."

I smile the sweetest smile I can muster. "What do you think I am?"

"A vampire," he responds. "If I tell you it's time to leave, we leave. No questions or arguments."

"Yes, Dad." Topher flips me off before grabbing my hand and leading me to the street below. A group of drunk tourists runs past. Run isn't the right word. They stumble past in total confusion.

"Where are they coming from?" he asks, looking in both directions.

"It sounded like it was that way." I point to an alley not far from Bourbon. We take off running, hoping to find the source of the sound. A few blocks away, smoke billows from the side of an older building. Muted screams echo off the walls, working their way toward our ears. Neither of us hesitates, and we head straight toward the chaos.

"Oh, my God," Topher whispers as we approach the destruction. A heavy wooden door is blown off its supports, lying across the narrow alleyway. "This isn't a lycan bar. It's a vampire place."

"What do you mean, vampire place?"

"One of the vampires from the city operates it. It's not a good place." We enter the smoke-filled room, and the smell of death hits me immediately.

"This is bad."

On our right stands what's left of an antique wooden bar. Bottles of alcohol are shattered, spilling their contents on the floor. A young man is lying on top of the bar, the lower part of his body is missing. On the other side of the room is what remains of a stage. The stripper pole is still perfectly in place and beside it, the remains of a young woman are scattered across the stage floor.

"This is definitely the work of the cult," I whisper.

"Did Viktor own this bar?" Topher asks, moving carefully through the remains.

"I don't think so." In front of me, I see the remains of the vampire who did own it. The head of Brian, the track suit wearing, creepy vampire, is sitting on a table-top. His eyes are open, and his mouth is frozen in a permanent scream. What remains of his body is sitting perfectly in the booth behind, still wearing his signature clothing.

"Who's that?" Topher moves next to me.

"Brian. I don't know his last name. He's one of the higher-level vampires in New Orleans."

"I think you mean, *was*. Why didn't he turn to ash?"

"That's an excellent question that I have no answer for. Maybe even the earth doesn't want him. Whoever did this made sure he was dead. They knew the explosion wouldn't kill him but decapitation would." I move closer to Brian's remains. The cut on his neck is clean, not from teeth, but from a weapon. "I don't think this was the cult."

"The council?" Topher asks the question I'm thinking.

"From the looks of this wound, it's from a sword or a long blade. This was done by someone who knew how to wield a blade." Topher's face looks at me in question. "It was part of my dissertation."

"It would make sense for it to be the council. Could there be more here than Hypatia?"

"God, I hope not." Sirens echo in the distance, and neither of us needs to be inside when humans arrive. Topher reads my mind, and we duck out of the building and into the surrounding bystanders.

"Look for anyone who looks out of place," he whispers as we slowly walk through the group.

"This is New Orleans. Everyone looks out of place." Topher keeps his hand around my arm as we walk through the crowd. On the other side of the group, I see a face that stops me in my tracks.

"What is it?" Topher looks in the same direction, not seeing anything.

I look again, and the woman is gone. "I...I saw someone that looked familiar."

We walk in the direction where the woman was standing. "Who was it?" I stare in disbelief at the spot where she stood, not sure if my mind is playing tricks on me. "Amelia? Who did you see?"

"Tammy. I saw my mother."

Topher turns me toward him. "Your mother? I thought she was…"

"Dead?" I finish his statement for him. "Yeah, she is."

We both scan the street. "Do you think that was her?"

"It couldn't be, could it?" I'm so confused.

"Do you know for sure that she's dead?"

"If you're asking if I saw the body, no. I was twelve. She just stopped coming home one day. I read in the newspaper about a body being found and that she had been identified as my mother." My mind plays through all the possible scenarios that could've happened, none of which make sense.

"Is it possible that she's still alive?"

"Yes, maybe. I don't know."

"Edon said she was able to wolf out. Maybe she's living with a lycan pack out of town somewhere."

"Why would she leave me alone?" Anger-filled tears flood down my cheeks at the realization that I have some deep-seated issue involving Tammy Sue Lockhart, or whatever the hell her name is.

"Because she was confused or lost? I don't know. Maybe that was just someone who looked like her. She's bound to have changed since the last time you saw her. That could've just been a look-alike. We all have one." Topher's attempt to lighten the mood isn't helpful.

"Maybe you're right," I lie.

"Of course, I'm right." He pulls his phone out, checking a text. "Edon just asked if we could come back to the bar for a meeting."

The sigh that leaves my lips is louder than the passing cars. "Is no an option?"

"Probably not."

The normal New Orleans bar crowd is gone, and the bar is filled with lycan as we enter.

"What the hell is a bloodsucker doing here?" a tall, older man spews as we enter.

"The same as you," I retort. "Edon asked me to come." I move in front of the lycanthrope, barely reaching his chest. "Have any more questions?"

"I asked Amelia to be here because this affects the vampire community as much as it does ours. With Viktor being...gone, she, along with a few who haven't arrived yet have been invited to represent their community. If you have a problem with it, Earl, feel free to leave."

Earl glares into my eyes, both of us refusing to back down. "Whatever," he snarls, backing against the wall.

The door opens, and three familiar faces enter. Violet, followed by Erick and Phillipe enter the door in what looks like a royal parade. Each one of them is perfectly dressed, with every hair in place. They look like a badass version of the Three Stooges. Violet smiles when she sees me. Looking around the room, there's a definite difference between the two groups. Most of the lycan are broad-chested and resemble lumberjacks, while the vampires look like they came from a photo shoot. My new friend behind me growls as they enter.

"I've asked Philippe, Violet, Erick, and Amelia to meet with us tonight. Something is happening in our town that must be stopped."

Phillipe and Erick nod, while Violet waves at the staring crowd. "Hello!" she says with a smile.

Grumbles are heard throughout the room. "Thank you, Edon, for the invitation. Normally, we don't get involved in human affairs, but one of our own was killed tonight," Erick smooth talks the crowd. "You're right when you say something is happening in our town. It's not just a lycan or vampire issue, it's an issue that we all must reconcile."

"What are you suggesting?" Edon asks.

"I believe the matter of what is to be done is better discussed between you and me," Phillipe answers for the group. "Nothing against the people in this room, but with everything that's happened, I'm sure you understand." The lycan begin to mumble their disapproval.

"With all due respect, Phillipe, this matter involves each one of us. It's apparent from tonight's attack that there are no limitations to who they're killing. Last time it was a lycan bar, tonight was a vampire establishment. None of us are safe." Phillipe concedes and steps against the wall.

"What the hell is out there?" the man behind me yells.

"We believe the cult is behind the attacks," Edon lies.

"I thought the cult was taken care of?" a younger lycanthrope asks from the other side of the room.

"Their leader was taken care of, but the cult has regained a new one." Edon pulls out the file he showed Topher and me a few days ago. "We have reason to believe their new leader is barely an adult." He shows the picture to the crowd.

Mumbles are heard throughout the room. "That's just a kid. He's harmless." A woman steps forward. She's wearing jeans and a sweater, and her hair is in a tight ponytail. "You can't tell me that kid orchestrated these two attacks."

"Darlene, if you have more information, please feel free to share it. As of right now, this is all we have to go on." She crosses her arms in defiance of Edon's words.

I step toward the middle of the room. "The vampire that was killed was beheaded with an extremely sharp sword."

Everyone in the room stares at me. "What are you talking about, Amelia?" Violet asks.

"Topher and I were close enough to hear the explosion. We got there before anyone else. When we did, I found Brian. He was decapitated by someone with knowledge of swordsmanship and weaponry."

"How the hell do you know that?" Earl shouts from somewhere behind me. "Those video games the young people play?" The lycan laugh at his words.

I turn, facing the man. "My doctorate is in European Mythology. Part of that degree was the study of weaponry craftsmanship from and since the medieval period. The cut that separated Brian's head from his body was clean, sharp, and precise." I've moved directly in front of the wolf, making him unnaturally nervous. I'm feeling rather bitchy tonight, and my new friend is the victim of that.

"Whatever, whore," he mumbles.

"You need to work on your comebacks, my friend." Topher's hand on my shoulder brings me back to reality, and I back away.

"What would that mean, Amelia?" Erick asks.

"I don't think anyone in the cult would have access or knowledge to be able to wield a sword of that caliber." I look around the room. "I believe there's someone or something else involved."

The vampires in the room look at me, and I know they're thinking the same thing I am. Hypatia and the council. To their benefit, no one voices their concerns.

"The question is, what are we going to do about it?"

"Nothing," the woman from earlier says. "They're not bothering me or mine. I say we leave them the hell alone, and they'll get bored."

These people are idiots.

"If you think they're going to get bored or leave us alone, you're dumber than your haircut." Violet steps into the center of the room. "This isn't going away. The sooner you people realize that, the better."

"What are you suggesting, bloodsucker?" a new voice yells.

"I'm suggesting we work together to figure out what this is and how we're going to stop it."

"I ain't working with no vamps," Darlene yells.

Edon crosses his arms across his chest. "As Alpha, I'm giving you no choice." He shifts forms in an instant. Standing in front of me is a black wolf, nearly six feet tall. He's both gorgeous and terrifying at the same time. He snarls, and the lycan in the room bow. Topher lets go of my shoulder and lowers to one knee. The only people left standing are the four vampires.

"We'll be in touch," Erick says as the three of them exit.

back at the haunted mansion

SINCE ARRIVING at Topher's loft, neither of us has said much about the meeting. Topher starts *The Chamber of Secrets*, and we resume our positions from earlier. It's not until the final credits roll that he breaks the silence.

"Do you think it's the council?"

I roll over in his arms. "At first, yes. Now, I'm not sure. What would be the purpose? Admittedly, I don't know much about the council, but I don't think their mission is to stir conflict around the world. From what I've gathered, they're in charge of finding vampires that break the rules and dealing with them. What would they gain from killing the very people they work to keep hidden from common knowledge?"

"The cult?" he asks.

"No. If you'd met Roger, you'd understand. He's a

kid with some serious issues. There's no way he would've been able to arrange all of this."

"Then who? We're running out of suspects."

I grab the spiral notebook I used to research my mother and tear that sheet from the metal fingers. "This mystery is solved. Let's start a new one." I draw my line and label them. "What do we know?"

"There's no rhyme or reasoning for who they kill," Topher answers.

"They're good with weapons," I add.

"That's it. That's all we know." Topher sits up, pushing me slightly off of his chest. My stomach growls with the movement. "We need to get you something to eat. Feel like taking a walk?"

"I have some in my loft. This will be my fifth bottle of the day."

"What's going on with you?" he asks, leading me to the door.

My phone buzzes in my pocket, and a message from Violet pops on the screen.

> We're meeting at LaLaurie Mansion.
> Bring the wolf.

"Looks like there's a change of plans." I pull Topher to a stop. "Want to go to a haunted house and meet with a bunch of vampires?"

Topher stares at me blankly. "This feels like some sort of trick question."

I laugh, dragging him out of the loft and toward the

ghostly tourist trap. We arrive in front of the haunted mansion ten minutes later. Even in the middle of the night, a group is stopped and taking pictures of the mansion. Their leader is talking about the horrors the owner inflicted on the people who lived there and how the screams can be heard coming from the house to this day. As soon as they step away, I enter the code, and we sneak inside.

"I'm not a huge fan of this," Topher announces, once inside. "The history of this house has always fascinated me but not enough to visit."

"It's not as bad as you'd think." I lead him to the back room where the other three are already waiting.

"Amelia!" Violet comes to my side and gives me an awkward side hug. The jury's still out on how angry I am with her. Instead of returning the hug, I smile.

"Have a seat, my dear." Erick stands as we enter. "It's lovely to see you again."

"This is Christopher St. James," I introduce my new friend to the group.

"Edon's son and future Alpha of New Orleans," Phillipe announces.

"Yes, sir. Thank you for the invitation."

Phillipe sits down, motioning for Topher to sit next to him. "This meeting is not meant to be disrespectful to Edon or the lycan. I wanted to meet with the leaders of our community to discuss what I'm sure you already have knowledge of."

"The council," Topher fills in the blank.

"The council," Phillipe confirms. "With Viktor's disappearance and Hypatia's appearance, this could be their work."

"Why would they kill Brian?" Erick asks. "I'll admit. Brian is high on everyone's kill list, but he hasn't done anything to warrant the wrath of the council."

"That we know of," Violet adds.

"Whoever killed him was a professional. Topher and I saw the body. There wasn't a scratch on him other than the clean slice through his neck." I look around the table with my words. "Brian would've been hard to kill. Whoever is responsible, didn't give him a chance to fight."

"Hypatia would know how to wield a sword," Erick confirms. "That leads us back to the question of purpose. Why kill Brian?"

"What if it's not the council and not the cult?" I ask.

"What are you saying, Amelia?" Violet asks.

I shrug. "I don't know. Maybe there's something new out there."

"Then that would suck balls," she answers. "We don't need a new threat."

"Where is Viktor?" Erick asks from across the table.

"I don't know."

"Normally, I wouldn't question someone's response, but this time I will. Where is he, Amelia."

I stand. "I don't know where he is. We went to Haiti to look for clues about Celeste and," I look down at my dirty shoes, "we're not a couple anymore. Hell, I'm not sure we ever were."

"What do you mean, clues about Celeste?" Erick stands, moving toward me.

"She left."

"She what?" his voice sounds like the predator he is.

Phillipe stands, matching Erick's energy. "She left. That's all you need to know. That's Viktor and Celeste's business, not ours."

"The bloody hell it isn't. Hypatia is here in town on behalf of the council, searching for the immortal child that Viktor's conveniently forgotten to tell us about all this time. No doubt he's gone wherever she is."

"Don't forget your place, Erick," Phillipe warns.

"My place? Who do you think you are to tell me of my place?"

Phillipe's appearance changes from a handsome French gentleman to a monster in a split second. He flies across the room, slamming Erick into the wall behind him and knocking a piece of plaster loose in the process. "With Viktor gone, I am the oldest vampire in New Orleans, which makes me the one who *can* tell you your place."

Erick hisses as he's pinned against the wall.

"I'll repeat myself once more." He releases his hold on the British vampire. "Don't forget your place, *Erick*."

Erick takes a moment to straighten the black sport coat and bright red tie he's wearing. "If you'll excuse me." He clears his throat before exiting through the front door. Topher's eyes are as large as saucers.

Phillipe sits back at the large table, his appearance back to normal. "Now, where were we?"

"Is there something out there that would be after both the lycan and vampire communities?" Violet asks the even smaller group.

Phillipe sits back in his chair. "Not that I'm aware of. But that doesn't mean, no. Harrison and Viktor are the ones with that knowledge, and since neither are around, we're at the mercy of whatever the hell it is."

"It has to be the council. Amelia's right. The cult doesn't have the ability to pull off what's been happening around here. The council does. Hypatia is the strongest vampire that any of us are aware of. You can't convince me she's not involved," Violet says, propping her feet on the antique table.

"Again, that leaves us with why she would target Brian?"

"Maybe she knew how much of an asshole he was?" she answers. "Hell, you'd have to be blind to miss it."

"What do you think Christopher?" Phillipe asks the wolf next to me.

Topher sits a little straighter. "Amelia and I were the first ones inside the bar after the attack. The building and everyone inside were completely destroyed. Human and vampire alike were killed for no other reason than being in the wrong location at the wrong time."

"The cult didn't care who they killed," Violet says. She turns toward Topher. "What are you thinking?"

He sighs and looks at me before answering. "I agree with Amelia. This was the work of something altogether different."

"Well, shit," she answers. "We needed some more excitement in our lovely city."

"The person or persons behind these attacks are acting from anger. They're not on some religious quest or punishing those around them. They're making a statement, and that statement is anger. They don't care who they hurt or who gets in the way."

Phillipe sucks in a deep breath. "Revenge can be a strong motivator."

"Who would be so angry at both communities that they wouldn't care who gets hurt in their quest for revenge?" I look around the room, hoping for an answer.

"That's what we need to find out," Phillipe answers. "In the meantime, I will keep Hypatia entertained." I don't want to think what that might entail. "Amelia, can you get in touch with Viktor or Celeste?"

"I don't know how to."

"Then you need to figure it out. We're going to need both of their help." Phillipe stands.

"What's the plan?" Violet asks the question that's on my mind, too.

Phillipe sighs. "I think we're stronger together. Especially since we don't know what we're up against."

"I'll talk to my father without the pack around." Topher moves in front of Phillipe and shakes his hands. "He's a reasonable man."

"I agree. Thank you, Christopher." Phillipe turns toward me. "Amelia, let me know when you contact Viktor."

I nod, not sure if he expects me to use carrier pigeons or telekinesis to find Viktor. Both will have the same amount of effectiveness at this point.

"How the hell does he expect you to find Viktor and Celeste?" Topher asks, once inside the safety of my loft. "Viktor has nearly a thousand years of stealth to rely on. Not to mention, he's protecting his daughter. He won't be found unless he wants to be found."

I collapse on the couch, thinking the same thing. "Maybe Viktor will be hidden, but what about Celeste?"

"What do you mean?" Topher collapses next to me.

"Celeste has a Ph.D. in computer science. She knows how to keep a low profile online." Topher turns toward me, waiting for me to continue. "I think I might know someone who can help us." I grab his hand. "Come on."

An hour later we're standing in front of one of Viktor's many properties in the city, a beautiful two-story brick home on the edge of the Flower District. Soft pink flowers fill the baskets underneath the heavily leaded windows, spilling out to the ground below. "Where are we?"

I ring the doorbell, and a familiar face appears as

the wooden door cracks open. "Amelia! I thought I sensed you," Fran exclaims the moment she sees me. "Does this mean Mr. Luquire has forgiven me?"

"Fran, this is my friend, Topher." She looks him up and down, judging him by his lycan blood.

She nods. "What kind of a name is that?"

"It's short for Christopher. Topher was my nickname as a kid, and it stuck." He smiles warmly at the middle-aged vampire in front of us.

"May we come in? I need your help." She turns back to me, and her smile returns.

"Of course, dear. Where are my manners?" The door opens, and we follow her inside the perfectly decorated home.

"This is beautiful." I run my fingers along the carved woodwork above the fireplace.

"It is. Mr. Luquire purchased this for me many years ago. He was always so good to me." She looks down at her words, wringing her hands together. "Please, have a seat." She motions to the Victorian couch in front of her. "Would you care for anything to eat, Amelia?" My stomach growls at her words.

"That would be great. I've been hungry today." Fran disappears into a swinging door, returning moments later with a large glass of blood.

"Now, how can I help you?" She sits in the chair across from us.

I finish off the blood and set the empty glass down with a thud. "Viktor has disappeared."

Fran laughs. "I'm not sure why you think I can help with that. I haven't heard from him since...since I left."

I slide forward on the couch. "Celeste is back."

"What? Is she okay?" Tears fill her eyes.

"She's more than okay." I smile. "She found a way to age herself. She's no longer a child."

Fran stares at me blankly. "How...how is that possible?"

"Voodoo, science? Truthfully, I don't know."

She stands, clapping her hands together. "Does that mean I can come home?"

"You're safer here for the moment. Hypatia has been staying at the Mandeville house."

"Hypatia?" she interrupts. "What is she doing here?"

"You know her?"

She laughs. "More like, know *of* her." She sits back on the chair. "She's here looking for Celeste, isn't she?"

"We think so."

"That's why he left." I nod. "Then I'm not sure how you think I can help you."

"Viktor is off of the map, but I believe Celeste isn't." Fran stares at me in anticipation. "You know her passwords and the places she visited while working on her degree. If anyone can find her, you can."

Fran takes a deep breath. "I'm not nearly as skilled as Celeste."

"You don't have to be as skilled. You just need to know how to find her."

"Follow me." She stands, leading us into a room that looks like it used to be a library. Shelves that used to hold books line the walls, now full of electronic equipment.

"What is this room?" Topher speaks for the first time.

"It's how I earn money." Fran smiles. "I offer quite a few services through my online businesses."

I laugh out loud. "I never would have imagined you with a room full of computers."

"While Celeste was earning her doctorate, I learned with her. Being a nanny for over three hundred years has its advantages."

She sits behind a large desk covered with computer monitors. "Let me do some research. I'll contact you the minute I uncover anything."

tammy o'connell

WHILE FRAN WORKS on finding Viktor, Topher and I head to one of my favorite places on earth, the library. "Why are we here?" he asks, following me through the high-arched windows.

"I want to research the city files more in-depth than I can online. Some libraries still have old newspapers in the basement."

An older woman greets us at the front desk. She gives Topher an approving eye and smiles before turning toward me. "How can I help you, young lady?"

"I'd like access to the archives, please."

The woman scribbles something on a piece of paper and hands it to me. "Take this to Elaine, on basement level 2."

"Yes, ma'am. Thank you." The elevator has a gate that lowers and raises at the same time. Once inside,

Topher pushes the button for the subbasement and flips the antique handle.

"This feels a little sketchy." He laughs awkwardly.

"You've watched too many movies."

He slides the doors open, revealing something straight from a Travel Channel documentary. Windowless gray walls greet us as we enter the room full of metal bookshelves.

"Can I help you?" an older white-haired woman asks, sliding her glasses off of her nose.

"Elaine?" Topher asks, turning on the charm.

"I'll be anyone you want." She smiles a wide smile with her words.

Topher hands her the paper the greeter gave us. "Are you looking for anything specific?" she asks.

"I'd like to see newspaper articles from the '50s to '70s." My words startle the woman who just now notices I'm there.

"That's a wide range, young lady. How about we start with the '70s and work our way back?"

"That's perfect. Thank you."

Elaine grunts, standing from her cluttered desk. "Have a seat over there." She points at a desk near the elevator door. "It'll take me a few minutes to gather them together." She winks at Topher before disappearing down one of the aisles.

"Did she wink at you?" I whisper.

"I think so." He laughs. "What can I say? Grandmas

love me. Are you going to tell me what we're looking for?"

"No, because I don't know." I sigh, sitting in a chair that rivals Elaine in age. "Anything strange that happened in the Quarter. Something similar to what's been going on but not current."

Elaine appears out of nowhere, setting a pile of wrapped newspapers on the desk. "This is 1979. Before I grab more, look through these, and let me know when you get close to needing more."

"Yes, ma'am. Thank you." I smile. She touches Topher on the shoulder before returning to her desk across the room.

I hand Topher half of the stack, and we begin gently turning pages, searching for anything that stands out. "Oh, look. Bread is going on sale next week for thirty cents. We should stock up."

"I don't think that's what we're looking for." Topher and I are getting close to the end of our stacks. I glance at Elaine to find her head slumped over, and she's sound asleep.

"Ms. Elaine?" Topher asks from our spot. She jumps up immediately.

"Yes, dear?"

"We're ready for more."

She jumps up from the desk. "I'll be right back." Several minutes pass before she comes back to our desk, setting another large stack of papers for us to explore. "This is 1978. If you'll tell me what you're looking for, I might be able to help. I've been down here long enough, I've read just about everything." She huffs a laugh. "I'm not joking."

"I'm looking for any unusual activity in the Quarter. Bombings, vigilante attacks, anything that stands out."

Elaine freezes in thought. Several minutes of awkward silence pass before she comes back to reality. "I have just the thing. I'll be right back."

"That was weird," Topher whispers as we watch the woman shuffle her way to the back. "It was like she had a glitch or something."

Elaine pops back at the desk, handing me a much smaller stack of papers. "Look for the September issue. I remember reading something about a bombing."

"You remember everything in here?" Topher asks.

"Not all of it. But I have been down here for many years." She laughs, leaving us with the stack.

Following directions, I pull out the September issue of *The Times-Picayune*. "This is from 1950." I scan the pages, not sure what I'm looking for.

"There." Topher points at a small article at the bottom of the last page. "21 Dead in Local Nightclub Bombing," Topher reads the headline out loud.

"It was the same club that was hit today." I read the address out loud.

"Are you sure?"

"One hundred percent." I sit back in my chair, not sure what one has to do with the other.

"Do you think that's a coincidence?" Topher asks.

"There's no such thing as a coincidence. Ms. Elaine?"

"Yes, dear?"

"Do you have any paper I could use to take notes on this?"

Elaine shuffles over, carrying paper and a pencil. "Anything else I can help you with?"

"No, ma'am. You've been more than helpful. Thank you."

Topher stacks all of our papers up and stands holding them. "Oh, I'll get those, dear."

"I'll carry them for you." Topher flashes his smile again.

She pushes my shoulder gently. "Hold onto this one, girl. He's a keeper."

Back in the solitude of the ancient elevator, Topher clears his throat. "I'm a keeper."

I can't hold back the laughter. "You're something, alright. I was getting worried that Ms. Elaine was going to jump your bones back there."

"What can I say?" He laughs, lifting the gates of the elevator for us to exit. On the way through the front door, a familiar face catches my eye. I stop in place. "What?" he asks.

The woman I saw from the bar is standing on the other side of the large glass windows that flank the street. "Do you see that woman?" I nod toward the image without taking my eyes off her.

"Yes," Topher answers. "Is that her?"

I don't care who sees me. I move vampire speed through the door and in front of the woman. "Who are you?" I spew.

The woman smiles, showing snow-white teeth. "That depends on who you think I am."

Topher runs out the door and moves to my side. She makes eye contact with him and smiles a wicked smile. "You're a big one."

"Who are you?" I repeat.

She turns her attention back to me. "Has it really been that long, Amelia?"

"I need to hear you say it," I whisper.

The woman smiles. "I think you know."

"Say it."

"I see you're just as demanding as you were as a child." I move at vampire speed, shoving her into the brick wall behind us, my teeth on full display.

"You left me. You deserted a twelve-year-old in the projects of New Orleans." I release my hold on her and refuse to cry. Topher stands back, giving me room to do whatever I need to do.

"If I'd have known you'd end up a bloodsucker, I would have killed you first."

I don't dare let her know how badly her words hurt. "At least I didn't kill the people that took care of me."

She stands straighter at my words. "It was an accident."

"Why are you here?"

"I've seen the errors of my ways. Maybe I want to reunite with my daughter."

"Your daughter doesn't want anything to do with you."

Tammy's eyes change from human to something I don't have words for. Topher steps closer to my side. Energy rolls off of him. "As the next Alpha of New Orleans, I'm asking you to get yourself in line."

She laughs. "You're nothing more than a boy, and you're not my Alpha. Mind your own damn business." She straightens the cropped-off T-shirt she's wearing and stands straighter. "I'll be in touch." She joins in with the crowd and disappears within seconds.

"Amelia?" Topher places his hand on my shoulder. "Are you okay?"

Am I okay? Truthfully, I don't know. I stare at the spot where Tammy stood moments earlier. "I want to go home." Topher laces his fingers through mine and leads me away from the busy street to the quietness of my loft. I don't remember getting home as he leads me to the couch, never letting go of my hand. He pulls me into his lap, wrapping his arms around me and pulling me to his chest, providing the comfort Tammy never did.

I don't know how much time has passed when Topher's stomach rumblings become louder than the self-pity flowing through my head. "We better get you something to eat before you die."

"I'm okay," he answers.

I pull away from his hold. "So am I. Thank you for being here when I needed you."

"It's what I do." He smiles.

I stand, pulling him up beside me. "Let's go grab some dinner." I head to the refrigerator, taking yet another bottle of blood out and downing it.

"Are you sure you're, okay? How much have you had to eat today?"

"I've lost count." I throw the bottle in the recycle bin. "I'm good now."

"We need to tell Edon and the vampires about Tammy."

"I know." I sigh. "Let's get you something to eat first. Maybe Fran will find a way to contact Celeste before then." My voice sounds sad, even to me. Topher wraps his arm around me, pulling me close as we head downstairs to the Quarter. He leads us to a small restaurant off the usual tourist paths. A few locals are scattered around the room as we enter. The only people here are human, and I'm grateful.

"What would you like to eat?" a young girl, not much older than me asks as she stares at Topher.

"I'll take a water, please," I answer, drawing her attention back to me.

"And you?" She continues to stare at Topher.

"I'll take a hamburger, rare, with extra cheese, please." He closes the menu and hands it back to her with a warm smile.

"Is that all?"

"Yes, please," he answers.

"If you need anything else, my name is Mandy." She walks away, shaking her backside more than when she walked up.

"Does that get old?" I ask.

"What?"

"Women constantly throwing themselves at you."

He turns, looking at the server. "Was she doing that?"

"You can't tell me you didn't notice that. She would've sat in your lap and licked your balls if you'd asked."

"Really?" He moves to stand. "Excuse me." He laughs.

"You better sit your ass down." I smile with my threat.

"Yes, ma'am." He slides back in his seat. A few minutes later, Mandy shows up with a huge hamburger and a plate full of fries.

"The fries are courtesy of me." She sets an unordered drink beside the plates, forgetting my water.

"Did you get my water?" I'm not going to drink it, but it's the fact of the matter.

Mandy turns toward me. Again, she's surprised by my existence. "Oh, I'm sorry. I'll get that for you."

"Still didn't notice?" I smirk.

Topher laughs a deep, sexy laugh. He reaches across the table, lacing his fingers through mine just as Mandy makes her way back to the table. "I can't believe we're having triplets! Can you imagine what the twins are going to think when we tell them?"

Mandy sets the water in front of me and leaves without another word. I can barely keep my laughter in control. "That was epic."

Topher eats the burger in record time and leaves the fries untouched. "Ready to go see Edon?"

"Not really."

"Yeah, me neither." I follow him out of the restaurant and down to the lycan bar. Edon's inside his office. From the looks of his clothes and hair, he hasn't been home for a while.

"What do I owe the pleasure of this visit?" His words are laced with sarcasm. He's clearly exhausted and tired of this entire ordeal. Join the club, Edon.

I look at Topher for support and take a deep breath. "I saw Tammy."

Edon stands. "You what?"

"I saw Tammy. The first time I saw her was after the attack at the vampire bar, and the second was at the library."

"You've seen your dead mother twice, and you're just now telling me?"

"The first time, I thought I imagined it. The second time didn't happen too long ago."

"Shit," he curses, throwing the paper he's holding on the desk. "Are you sure it was her?"

"We had a whole ass conversation. I'm sure."

"What did she say?"

I scoff. "Not much other than if she knew I was going to end up a vampire, she would've killed me instead of abandoning me. She said she'd be in touch."

"What the hell does that mean?" Edon asks.

"It means she's not going to be in contention for 'World's Best Mom,' and this shit show is only just beginning."

i tried

WE ENDED up at my loft after our revelation to Edon. Topher's been asleep on my bed for the past few hours, and I've read an entire vampire book series on a Kindle I found in one of the drawers. Instead of vampires that sparkle, this one is geared toward adults and has more sex scenes than anything else.

Reading these scenes not far from a gorgeous lycanthrope that is not opposed to getting in my pants has proven to be a huge distraction. I've had to stop myself several times from crawling in bed beside him. The sun is rising over the horizon just as the realization of my world crashes down.

Tammy is alive. My mother is alive.

I don't know whether to rejoice or curse her name. How could she abandon me, her child? I wasn't even a teenager yet when she left me for who knows what. I thought it was Harrison, but now, I'm not convinced.

What kind of a mother leaves her twelve-year-old daughter...alone?

"You're staring at me," Topher's voice is full of sleep as he raises his arms high, sending the sheet low on his abdomen.

"Sorry. I was lost in thought."

He flips the covers back and pats the empty space beside him. He's wearing nothing but a pair of boxer briefs that are several sizes too small for the package he's shoved inside them. "I promise I'll keep my hands to myself." He smiles a sexy smile that tempts me for more than just a cuddle.

I climb beside him, pressing my back against his chest as he wraps his arms around me, making me the little spoon. The intimacy from our connection is just what I need. I wiggle my way backward until every part of his body meets every part of mine. Topher moans as my ass rubs against him. "Sorry," I whisper.

"I'm not." His voice is deep and raspy on the back of my neck. Soft kisses elicit small gasps from my lips. Topher doesn't end his assault. He works his way from my neck to my shoulder in slow, warm kisses. "You taste so good."

I resist the urge to say something sarcastic and allow him to continue, working his way to my ear and earlobe. "Topher," I warn.

"What?" he growls in my ear. My eyes shoot open, and I turn, facing him.

"Did you just growl at me?" He slides his finger

under my chin, lifting my face even with his. His lips are on mine before I know what's happened. Our kisses begin gently, exploratively, and softly. Kissing a wolf is different than kissing a vampire. Viktor was an amazing kisser, but the heat coming from Topher and his kisses makes me crave more.

Using superhuman strength, I flip the giant lycanthrope to his back, straddling his hips and pinning his arms to the side of his body. "Amelia? What are you doing?" Instead of answering, I reach down, pulling my T-shirt and bra off in a move that would make a porn star applaud. His eyes switch from my mouth to my breasts. "God, you're beautiful."

Topher gently takes my nipple into his mouth, making me moan louder than I should've. Encouraged by my response, he cups the other with his hand, gently rubbing its twin with his thumb. My back arches in response. Evidence of his arousal is touching me in all the right places. I reach between us, wrapping my hand around his massive erection, and Topher stops his assault on my breasts.

"Are you sure about this? What about not jumping in bed with the next creature?" His voice is breathy.

"Fuck that." I pull the tiny boxer briefs down, exposing every inch of him. What awaits me is not what I expect. In fact, I'm not sure I've seen one this large...ever.

Topher flips our position, putting me on the bottom as he gently slides off the pair of sweatpants I put on last night. I have never been so turned on in my life. Once my pants are off, I lay naked and exposed in front of Topher, my only friend. "What?" I pant.

"I'm enjoying the view." He slides down, switching back and forth between each thigh, and kisses his way toward where I really want him to be. Pulling my legs over his shoulders, he doesn't waste a minute finding the softest part of me. The moment his mouth makes contact, I nearly leap off the bed. Digging into the covers beside me, I'm drawn into the cusp of pure ecstasy within minutes. I've had orgasms before, but nothing like this. My body lifts off the bed as he continues his combination tongue and sucking action. My entire body shutters as I come down from the high.

"Oh, my God. What kind of magic was that?" I ask between pants.

"Wolf magic," he answers, sliding up my body until the largest part of him is lined up where my body craves it.

"I was always Team Jacob, anyway."

Topher laughs as he gently enters my body, one inch at a time. "Is this, okay?"

"No. You're going too slow."

He continues to slide into me until there's nothing else left. The fullness of him is almost too much to contain. "Still, okay?" he whispers.

I don't answer, just begin slowly moving, forcing him to move with me. It doesn't take long for him to join my rhythm, and we move together in a choreographed dance that's been around for millennia. I wrap my legs around his waist, giving him as much access as possible. He lowers his lips to mine, matching the intensity of his thrusts, and within seconds I feel the coil forming deep inside. Topher's breathing has sped up along with the intensity of movement.

My body turns to putty in his hands as we explode together. Both of us cry out from the connection, and he collapses on the bed beside me. It takes a few minutes to regain control of my breathing.

"That was..." he's breathing too hard to talk.

"I agree," I answer.

He pulls me to his front, wrapping his massive body around mine as his erection presses into my back. I reach behind me, wrapping my hand around his thick appendage, and he sighs once more. He's clearly ready for round two, and I'm not going to wait. This time, I take control.

I flip him to his back and, straddling his hips, lower myself onto him slowly until our skin meets. He sits up, pulling our chests close together and wrapping his arms around each thigh. He picks me up, sliding me up and down slowly. "No, I want to be in control." I shove him flat on the bed as I continue moving slowly. Lifting almost to the tip and slowly sliding back down until there's no space between us. I stare him in the eyes as I move painstakingly slow.

It doesn't take long for the tension to build deep inside. Topher is breathing hard too, telling me he's as close as I am. He reaches behind me, grabs my ass, and squeezes at the same time the tension releases through my body. His body releases moments later, followed by a soft howl.

I can't control the smile that comes with the sound. "Did you just howl?"

"Maybe," he pants. "Sorry."

"Don't apologize. It was cute."

"Cute?" He smiles. "I can assure you there will be more than howls if you keep doing what you did."

I roll off of him and curl up beside him. "Thank you," I whisper.

He turns to me with a huge smile. "It's me who should be thanking you. That was perfection."

"You're kind of perfection." That was dumb. Why did I say that?

Topher doesn't seem to notice. He pulls me close and kisses me on the tip of my nose. "You're perfection." My stomach growls, interrupting the moment. "Hungry?"

"Starved," I answer.

"Like yesterday?"

"I'm not sure yet, but I am hungry." Topher slides out of bed, and I watch as the picture of perfection saunters across my loft to the refrigerator. There isn't an ounce of fat on his body, and with him naked, I can see the hint and curve of every muscle.

He returns with a bottle of goat blood, seconds later. "Why are you smiling?"

"I was just enjoying the view," I repeat his words from earlier. He waits until I drink the entire bottle before sliding in beside me.

"I could get used to waking up like this," he whispers into my neck.

"I can make that happen." Across the room, my phone begins to ring.

"Ignore it." He pulls me closer.

"I can't. What if it's Celeste or Fran or, God forbid, Tammy?" I slide out from the warmth of his arms and answer.

"Hello?"

"Amelia?" Fran's voice answers on the other side. *"I've found a way to contact Celeste."*

"We'll be right there." I turn to see Topher sliding on a pair of sweatpants and an oversized hoodie. God, he's hot. Staring at him fully dressed, just knowing what lies underneath the layers of fleece makes me want to go for round three.

"Where are we going?"

"Fran found a way to contact Celeste," I answer as I move back toward Topher.

"You might want to get dressed first. I mean, I'm okay with you going like that, but Fran might be weirded out."

I step in front of him, not caring that I'm completely exposed. I stand on my tiptoes, pulling his face to mine, and kiss him on the lips. He slides one hand behind my neck, pulling me closer, and the other on my cheek.

"You are amazing," he whispers into my mouth. "You need to stop kissing me unless you plan on finishing this before we leave." I reach both hands around, grabbing his cheeks and squeezing before heading into the bathroom to clean up and get dressed.

Thirty minutes later, we're in my BMW heading to the Flower District. Topher hasn't taken his hand off mine since we've left. It doesn't take long before we park in front of the beautiful home. Fran is at the door before we knock. "Good morning!" She looks between the two of us. "You two look like you've had a good morning."

I feel the blood rush to my cheeks at her words. "You found a way to contact Celeste?" I change the subject.

"I did." We follow her into the computer room where she climbs into the chair behind the desk. "This is a server that Celeste would use when she was working on her degree." She points to one of the three monitors on her desk. "I've been monitoring it for usage the past few days and finally got a hit this morning."

"Fran, I'm going to need you to explain this like I'm in kindergarten." She laughs at my words.

"To simplify it, Celeste is the only one with the ability to alter this page."

"And it's been altered," Topher fills in the blank.

"What if someone else has gotten her information and changed it? It could be anyone."

"Except it's not. Celeste is the only one with knowledge and information to do this site," Fran answers. "I can send her a message through this site, and I'm certain she'll get it. All I need to know is what you want me to tell her."

"Tell her to contact me. Tell her it's an emergency that can't wait."

Fran begins feverishly typing. "Done," she announces several minutes later.

"How will you know if she sees it?" Topher asks.

"She'll call Amelia." We turn to leave the room. "Amelia? I don't know what's going on and wouldn't pretend to know, but I'm here if you need me. These old bones still have some fight left in them."

"Thank you, Fran."

"What's the next step?" Topher asks, pulling away from the curb. "There are more plots to this insanity than I can keep up with."

"You and me both. One drama at a time. I'm going to check in with Phillipe and find out what's going on with Hypatia, then let's go see Edon. In case you forgot, Hypatia's timeline for my eminent death is coming quickly."

"No way in hell I'm letting that happen." Topher puts his hand on my thigh protectively.

an impromptu trip to florida

ON THE WAY to the lycan's unofficial headquarters, I send a nondescript text to Phillipe. Minutes later I receive an answer that makes my stomach sour.

> He's busy at the moment.

No doubt, Hypatia sent that text, meaning he's doing his part of keeping her occupied. I throw up a little in my mouth at the image that comes to mind.

"What's up?" Topher asks from the driver's seat.

"Phillipe is sacrificing for the good of us all." I shove my phone in my pocket, sending him warm wishes.

Several minutes pass before we park in front of the bar. "Does Edon sleep here?" It seems that he's here constantly.

"Most of the time," Topher answers. "After Mom

died, his way of coping was by ignoring his sons and throwing himself into being Alpha."

This is the first time I've heard Topher say anything negative about his father. I resist the urge to apologize for Edon's behavior. One of my toxic traits is feeling responsible for everyone around me and their happiness. A leftover side effect of childhood trauma, I suppose.

Edon is sitting at his desk and is wearing the same clothes as yesterday. He smiles weakly as we enter. "What's going on, Dad?" Topher sees the exhaustion on his father's face.

"Topher, Amelia. Any news?"

"Fran found a way to contact Celeste. She sent her message to contact me, this morning," I answer.

"That's great."

"What's going on with you?" Topher asks, stepping closer to his father's desk. "You look like you've been here for about a week. To be honest, you smell the same."

Edon runs a hand through his messy hair. "I've been researching Tammy." He looks at me when he speaks. "You're right. She's alive, and I've found information on where she's been for the past twelve years."

His words knock the wind out of me. "Where?"

"Florida," he answers. "The Everglades, to be more specific."

All I know about the Everglades are alligators and

mosquitos the size of my head. "What's in the Everglades?"

"A group of hybrid lycan."

"What?" Topher asks, not sure he heard correctly.

Edon leans back in his office chair. "There's a group of hybrids, living together in a small cluster."

"I thought hybrids rarely survive," I ask, recalling the information he shared earlier.

"They do, or that's what we believed."

"What does this mean?" I sit in the chair opposite Edon.

He scoffs. "It means we were misinformed."

"What does it mean for Tammy? Why is she here?"

"That, I don't know. You'll have to ask her."

"Could Tammy or the hybrid pack be responsible for what we thought was the cult?" Topher asks the perfect question.

"That's what I'm working on now." Edon sighs, flipping through pages scattered on his desk, pulling a piece of paper from a stack of others, and handing it to me.

I glance over a printout from a website discussing the destruction of vampires and lycan. "What is this?"

"The hybrids. A member of our pack is particularly skilled at the dark web. After a deep dive, he found their information." He shuffles through a few more pages, handing me another page. "There's more." I study the picture of the woman on the printout. Tammy's picture stares back at me. "Tammy's their leader."

"Let me get this straight." I stare at the Alpha of New Orleans. "My mother, Tammy O'Connell is a hybrid wolf who is the leader of an entire pack of hybrid wolves who want all vampires and lycan dead?"

"That sums it up quite well."

"Were they behind the previous cult?" Topher asks, sitting on the seat next to me.

"Not directly, but yes. From what I've discovered, Penelope was the money while this group was the one pulling the strings from afar."

"What does this mean?"

"It means Tammy is here to finish what the cult started and is responsible for the attacks in the Quarter on both of our groups."

"Hypatia had nothing to do with it?"

Edon shakes his head. "I don't believe so."

I stand, heading toward the door. "Are you coming?"

Both men stand, following me out the door. "Where are we going?" Topher asks.

"We're heading to the college." I climb into the driver's seat of my BMW and drive the two large men to the college campus where I met the new cult leader.

I park in Viktor's spot in front of the dorm building. "You're going to get a ticket," Topher says, climbing out of the back seat. I ignore him and head straight into the lobby. A young girl exits the locked door to the dorm rooms and stops in her tracks, staring at the two gorgeous lycan in her dorm lobby.

"Thank you." I smile, passing through the open door to the rooms. She clears her throat and mumbles a response as she hurries through the door, still staring at Topher.

"Amelia?" Edon whispers. "Are you going to tell me what we're doing?"

I bang on the door at the end of the hall. "We're paying Roger a visit."

"What if this isn't his room anymore?"

"Then we're breaking and entering." I bang even louder. "Roger, open the damn door!"

"Who is it?" a familiar voice calls through the closed door.

"Open the door, or I'll open it for you."

The door cracks open with the chain still in place. "Why are you here?"

I push the door, breaking the chain on impact. Roger is wearing pajamas with bunny rabbits covering them. The twin-size beds are pushed together, making a king-sized bed in the middle of the room. "This is the cult leader?" Edon makes the connection.

Topher looks the young man up and down. "This is their leader?"

Roger waves. "I don't know what you want, but I have class in thirty minutes."

Edon closes the hallway door, locking the four of us in the room. "Tell us about the cult." He's in full alpha mode, and his energy fills the room.

"I don't know what you're talking about," Roger stutters over his words.

"Oh, cut the bullshit, Roger. You were there, at their meetings. You volunteered to be an angel, for God's sake."

"I went to a few meetings, but when Greg died, they disbanded." He looks at the two lycan as he speaks.

"Let's try that again." Edon pulls a photograph of Roger up on his phone. "This is their new leader, and he remarkably looks like you."

"What?" Roger takes his phone, studying the screen. "That's me. I'm not the leader of anything."

"Tell me why you're listed as the leader." I move closer to the scared college student.

"I...I don't know. A lady from the national organization of the cult came to speak to me a few weeks ago. Maybe she thought I was the leader."

"What lady?" Topher asks the question I already know the answer to.

"She...she was tall and had light brown hair. I don't know who she was. She said she was interviewing me for their records on the group."

"Did she tell you her name?" Edon asks.

"No. She asked me a few questions about vampires and left."

I move inches from Roger's face and flash my teeth. "Do we look stupid enough to believe that story?"

The front of his pajamas becomes wet with urine as he physically shakes in response. "I'm not lying. She asked a few questions and left. I...I never heard from her again. I don't know why they're using my picture." I know without asking, he's telling the truth. He doesn't know anything else. I back away, pulling my teeth into my gums.

"We'll be in touch," I whisper as the three of us disappear as quickly as we appeared.

Back in the safety of my car, Edon laughs a deep belly laugh. "Why was that so much fun?" Topher joins his laughter as we pull away from the illegal parking spot.

"Why would Tammy use Roger's picture as the face of the cult?" I ask once the laughter dies down.

"Because he's easy and unassuming. He's the perfect human decoy." Edon answers.

"What's the purpose of a human decoy?"

"Distraction," I answer.

"We need to find Tammy." Topher leans forward from the back seat.

"We could go to the Everglades," I announce.

"I can have a jet ready in thirty minutes." Edon pulls his phone out of his pocket and begins making calls as I drive toward the airport.

Exactly thirty minutes later, we're loading the private jet and heading toward the Everglades. I'm disappointed when Sophie's not on board. In fact, there's no one besides the pilot as we board the small jet. "Our flight should take less than an hour," our unnamed pilot announces over the loudspeaker. Topher sits in the seat next to me as Edon sits a few rows ahead. Within minutes of liftoff, both men fall asleep, and I continue reading the vampire series on my tiny phone screen. It's a good thing I have vampire vision. The writing is so small, I'm not sure I'd be able to see it otherwise.

Not long after, the plane begins to descend, and we land at a small rural airport not far from the Glades. Topher jumps awake as we make contact with the ground below. My stomach growls loudly, evidence of my lack of food for the past few hours.

"Are you okay?" Topher whispers.

"Just hungry again."

"Maybe we can find blood here. How does alligator blood sound?" He laughs.

"Gross," I answer truthfully.

"Do we know where we're going?" I ask Edon as we exit the jet and move toward an awaiting Uber.

"The compound is off the grid, but I researched it before we left." He pulls his phone back out. "We'll need to charter an airboat. They're in the middle of what looks like water."

The Uber takes us to a nearby boat rental, abandoning us in the middle of a gravel parking lot. "This is weird."

We walk to the first boat docked. An older man greets us on approach. His body is bent over with age, and the overalls he's wearing have holes scattered throughout the legs. "We need to get to this location." Edon shows the man the GPS on his phone.

He laughs. "Ain't nothin' out there but gators and swamp. Why do you want to go there?"

"A friend of mine has a home there."

The man laughs for a second time. "I'm tellin' you, there ain't nothin' out there."

"We'd like to see for ourselves," Topher adds.

"Good luck with findin' a boat." He turns to walk away.

I move in front of him, looking him in the eyes. "You're going to take us to this location."

He blinks rapidly. "I'm goin' to take you to this location," he repeats my words.

"You're not going to ask us any questions or tell anyone what you see when we get there." He repeats my words in his mash-up of accents. "We'll wait here while you get the boat ready." The man turns, heading toward his boat.

Edon laughs. "I've never seen that done in person."

"Did you compel him?" Topher asks.

I shrug. "I don't know what to call it, but it worked."

"That's what you did to me in Jamaica, wasn't it?"

I clap my hands, changing the subject. "Looks like the boat is ready." We board the small airboat, and the confused look on our captain's face makes me feel guilty for the compulsion. He steers us out of the small marina toward the dot on the GPS.

The Everglades are beautiful and mysterious all at the same time. Large cypress trees grow in the middle of nowhere, seemingly from the water itself. The wildlife we pass is beautiful. Several smaller alligators scurry away, heading toward the safety of a nearby bank. Evidence of old homesteads remains in some of the trees. A few of them are still standing and look uninhabitable.

Topher laces his long fingers through mine, pulling our joined hands to his lips and kissing my hand gently. He knows this isn't easy for me, and I appreciate the gesture. The airboat begins to slow as we approach a large growth of cypress trees.

"This is the location," our captain announces as he slows to a complete stop. We drift into the trees seeing nothing that looks like the secret lair of lycan hybrids. "I told you there wasn't anythin' here."

"Take us around the entire area," Edon instructs. The man follows directions, weaving us in, out, and through the cluster of trees.

"That's strange," our captain announces. "I ain't never noticed that buildin' before."

"Take us there." I stand, moving to the front of the boat. He pulls up to what looks like a small dock and stops. The building is small and made from the same trees we're surrounded by. The tin roof is shiny and glistens in the Florida sun.

"This has to be it," Edon steps off the boat and onto the dock.

"Take one more step, wolf, and I'll blow your goddamn head from your body." Edon doesn't move. An older man steps out of the shack, pointing a shotgun in our direction. "What the hell do you want?"

I don't waste a second. I move faster than he can track, coming behind him and pulling the gun out of his hands. I have him pushed against the wall of the shack with my hand around his neck before he has time to process what happened. "Who are you?"

The man spits in my face. "Ask them, vamp." I turn to see Topher and Edon slammed against the dock with a group of men and women standing over them with guns pointed. We just walked into a trap.

insatiable thirst

I RELEASE my captive and back away. "This isn't necessary," I yell to the group. "We're not here to harm anyone, only to ask questions."

"What would a vampire and two lycan be doing together in the Glades?" my former captive spews. "From the looks of them, those two aren't your run-of-the-mill wolves. I'm guessing an alpha and his offspring."

"We're here because of my mother." The man turns his attention back to me.

"Your mother? Do any of us look like your mother?" The small group laughs at his words. "What's your mother's name? I'll keep an eye out for her. Although, we don't get many visitors here in the swamps."

"I can see why." I glare at the man. "My mother is Tammy Lockhart."

The man's face changes in an instant. "Tammy?" He

studies my face, looking for clues of the truth. "Your lies won't work here, bloodsucker."

"She's not lying," Topher yells from the dock. "Her mother is Tammy O'Connell-Lockhart, and she's a hybrid."

"We're all hybrids, boy," the man yells back. "Why do you think they were able to overpower you?"

I turn toward the man, looking him in the eyes. "You will release them and tell me what you know about my mother."

The man's face changes to serious as his eyes grow large. "I will keep them held captive and not tell you shit." The group behind me laughs hysterically. "I'm a hybrid, girl. You clearly don't know what all that entails. You can't use compulsion on me. I'm immune to your bullshit."

"Why don't you enlighten us?" I ask, focusing on keeping my voice calm.

"If dear old Tammy is your mommy, why don't you ask her?"

"Because she abandoned me when I was a kid. I haven't talked to her since," I lie.

"Then how'd you know to come here and look for her?"

I shrug. "Call it a hunch."

The door to the cabin opens and a young girl, no older than four or five, exits. She's wearing a dress and carrying a worn-out rag doll. "Daddy, what's going on?"

"Becky, get back inside." The girl turns to follow directions.

"Becky?" I call to her. She turns, staring at the spectacle in front of her. Her hair is a tangled mess, and the dress she's wearing is covered in dark stains. I stare into her eyes and recognize them instantly. They're mine. We have the same eyes.

"Shut up, vamp. Don't talk to her."

"Who is she?" Becky asks, moving toward me.

"She's nobody, baby. Go back inside. Daddy will be there in a minute."

"Where's your mother?" I ask the girl.

"She's gone. Why do you smell funny?"

The man moves quickly behind the girl and picks her up. "She's not safe to be around. Get back in the house." I could rush him while he's holding her, but that would risk the safety of Topher and Edon who still have guns pointed at their hearts. I don't have to ask to know they're loaded with silver bullets.

The man comes back outside, empty-handed. "She's Tammy's daughter, isn't she? She's my sister."

"I'm not answering any of your questions. Get the hell out of here before we kill all three of you."

"Are you sure you're prepared for that? You're right when you said he was an alpha. He's not just any alpha..."

"Amelia," Edon warns.

I ignore his warning and continue. "That man is Edon St. James, Alpha of New Orleans and one of the strongest of his kind. If you harm him or his son, you will not only bring the wrath of his pack but the wrath of packs from around the entire southern United States. Are there enough hybrids to handle that?"

For the first time, the man looks nervous, encouraging me to continue my verbal war. "My maker is the most powerful vampire on the continent, and guess who happens to be her favorite? That's right, the bloodsucker standing in front of you. If you harm any of the three of us, not only this small group of hybrids you have here but also Becky will die or worse."

"What do you want?"

"Tell me about Tammy." The man looks at his feet, clearly in an argument with himself internally. "I promise we will never let anyone know of your existence, and you will never hear from us again."

The man nods, and the group behind me puts their weapons away. Both Topher and Edon are on their feet instantly, and from the looks on their face, they're ready to kill. "Come inside." The three of us follow him inside the small shack with the remaining hybrids standing guard outside the door. "Go outside, Becky," the man demands as we enter.

On the way outside, Becky stops and looks me in the eyes. "You look like Mommy."

I smile warmly. "Your mother must be very beautiful then."

"Why are you here?"

"I'm looking for your mommy."

"She's gone."

I lean forward. "I'm sure she'll be back. She must have something really important to do if she left." The words hit hard. They're the same words I told myself over and over every day, until those days turned into weeks, months, and eventually years.

Becky hugs her filthy doll tightly. "I like you."

"I like you, too," I whisper. She exits the cabin and sits on the dock, overlooking the murky swamp water.

"Tammy's gone," my new friend answers.

"Why?" Edon asks. Anger still pours from his body as he takes up a ton of space in the small cabin.

"She left a few months ago. She went to New Orleans." The three of us share a knowing look.

"Again, why?" Edon repeats his question.

The man sits back, crossing his arms over his chest. "Tammy has a special...ability."

"What kind of ability?" Topher asks.

"She can shift forms."

Topher makes eye contact with me, knowing our discussion of her killing her foster father.

"When Becky was born," he sighs before continuing. "When Becky was born, Tammy knew she had the ability, too."

I turn toward the door. "Becky can turn into a wolf?"

"Not completely. However, that may change when she hits puberty."

"Why would that cause her to leave?" I ask.

"She went looking for her family."

I stare at the man in front of me. "Why do I feel like you're leaving an important part of this story out?"

He slides forward in his seat. "She wanted to kill everyone responsible for her ability." He rubs the side of his head. "I love Tammy, but she changed after the birth. She became obsessed with vampires, lycan, and their destruction."

"Is that why she went to New Orleans?"

"Yes." He nods. He moves toward an old computer in the corner of the cabin. "When she learned about the cult in New Orleans, she used that information to create a new one and recruited a new leader. She left not long after and hasn't been in contact. I don't know what happened from there." He hands me the laptop. "Any information she found will be on here. Take it. I don't want anything to do with it."

"I'm sorry," I whisper. There I go again, apologizing for something that has nothing to do with me.

"Me, too," he answers.

"Becky's beautiful."

He looks lovingly out the window. "She's going to need more than me when she gets older."

I grab a sheet of paper and pen, writing my name, phone number, and address on it. "When that happens, contact me. I'll help in any way I can."

He takes the paper and reads my name aloud. "For what it's worth, thank you."

"For what it's worth, you're welcome." The three of

us stand, moving toward the door. "Are we going to have any problems from the hybrids once we leave this cabin?"

"No. You have my word. I apologize about the whole gun thing."

Outside the cabin, I sit next to Becky, who has her feet hanging over the edge of the dock. "My name is Amelia."

"It's nice to meet you, Amelia."

I touch the scraggly hair of her doll. "Your doll is beautiful, just like you."

She giggles. "I wish her hair looked like yours." I subconsciously pull my hair forward and am met with bright red curls.

"It's not as pretty as yours."

"Will you come back?" Becky asks.

"I don't know if I'll come back here, but I'm sure we'll see each other again. I can tell you are super smart."

"Daddy says I'm scary smart."

I laugh at her words as I stand. Our airboat is still in the same spot, and our captain has the same glazed-over look in his eyes. "Thank you," I say to the small group of hybrids standing on the docks. "We will keep your secret."

Becky runs back to her dad's leg, holding on tightly as we load the boat and pull away from the dock. The three of us don't speak again until we're loaded back into the safety of the jet.

"That was eventful," Topher says as we lift into the sky. His words start a spontaneous giggle that takes five minutes to resolve between the three of us.

An hour later, we land back in New Orleans. Our entire trip to the Everglades of Florida and back again took less than eight hours. The sun is beginning to set in the sky, and my stomach is growling louder than usual.

We drop Edon back at the bar and head back to the safety of my loft. The three of us didn't discuss a plan or possible outcome from what we learned today, once we left the Glades. Between the trauma of the day and learning the truth about the hybrids, no one brought any possible future outcomes up for discussion.

Topher opens the door to my loft, and I follow him inside. My stomach growls so loudly it hurts. I double over in pain. "Amelia? What's going on?"

"I'm really hungry."

He rushes to my refrigerator looking for a bottle of goat blood. "Do you have any more blood? There's none in here."

I lay down on the couch, hoping to ignore the insatiable thirst brewing inside. "No, I don't think so."

"What can we do?" He moves back to my side.

I cover my mouth to hide the fangs that have popped out without warning. "I don't know. I need to find something to eat."

"What about a cat or something? I'm sure there's one around the Quarter I can find."

"No. Cats are so small I might kill it."

The hunger pain strikes again, and I curl my legs to my chest in response. "We have to do something. I won't sit here and watch you suffer."

"I'll be okay. It'll pass." My words are forced. He heads to the kitchen and returns moments later with a knife. "Stabbing me might take the pain away." I try to make light of the situation. "Make sure you hit my heart."

"That's not funny." He puts the knife to his wrist and makes a small slit.

"No! I may not be able to stop."

"I trust you," he whispers. "You won't hurt me."

"*I* don't trust me." He doesn't give me an option. His wrist is on my lips, and I'm unable to ignore the blood-lust that comes with it. I latch on, pulling the sweetness of his blood as it enters my body. I moan as it fills my stomach, stopping the pain immediately.

"Amelia?" he questions, trying to pull his arm away. I ignore the voice and continue drinking. "Amelia, that's enough." His voice echoes through the back of my mind. "Amelia!" I'm drawn back to the present as the reality of what I'm doing hits me. I release his arm and back away into the recesses of the couch. Topher moves to the kitchen, grabbing a towel and wrapping it around the injury.

"Are you okay?" I whisper as he comes back to my side.

"I'm fine. You didn't hurt me."

"Are you dizzy or feeling sick at all?"

He laughs. "No, I'm fine. Are you okay?"

I relax as he smiles. "I feel better than I have in a long time."

"It's my magical blood. I'm going to wrap this up." I watch as he disappears into the bathroom. What just happened? I smile at the warmth that fills both my stomach and my heart.

we need a plan

TOPHER SLIDES between me and the back of the couch, wrapping me in his long arms. "Can we stay like this forever?"

I turn, facing him. "As much as I'd like that, we have the reality of our world pounding down on top of us. We need to talk about what happened today."

"Do we have to?" he whines, making me smile.

"I can't stop thinking about Becky," I admit. "She's my sister, and Tammy deserted her the same way she did me."

"It seems her personal vendetta takes precedence over her kids." Topher's words hit hard. He's right, but hearing it from someone else is harder than the voice that stays on repeat in my head. "She'll be fine. She has her father and a support system. That's more than you had."

"If Tammy is the one behind the cult, that takes

away one of our threats. Roger is no more than a face behind her revenge." I lay my head on his shoulder, trying to get as close as possible. The warmth radiating from him feels amazing.

"If the hybrid was correct, Tammy has a vendetta out for anyone who has done her wrong, or at least, by her perception done her wrong."

"I have no doubt Harrison hurt her." Flashes of Harrison chasing me through the basement come to mind. "But she's half lycanthrope. Why would she be after them?"

Topher shrugs. "Maybe she has abandonment issues? Maybe something happened after she killed my grandfather."

"Maybe I can help her."

Topher pulls away, making eye contact with me. "Help her how?"

"Help her realize killing every vampire and lycan in the city isn't going to solve her problems."

Soft lips touch my forehead. "I know you well enough to know you feel a huge responsibility to save the world, but Tammy holds pain that is beyond your scope. If she would leave her daughters to seek revenge, there's no reasoning with her."

"I have to try."

"Then I'm here to help you any way I can."

I flip him on his back and straddle him in one quick move. "Do you know how hot you are?"

"Is this a trick question?" He smiles.

I rest my head on his chest. The rhythmic beating of his heart sends comfort through my body. "What are we, Topher?"

"What do you mean?"

"I mean, are we just a young vampire and her future alpha protector, or are we...?" I don't finish my sentence.

Topher puts both hands on my head and gently lifts my face until our eyes meet. "We're whatever you want us to be."

"You're the future alpha. You're supposed to populate the city with cute little wolf babies." I pause. "Vampires can't have children."

"I don't care about any of that. The future is just that, the future. Right now, I'm where I want to be, here with you, and I have no plans on that changing any time soon."

"I'll have to admit, you're growing on me." From the feeling between my straddled legs, that's not the only thing that's growing.

"I have that gift." He lifts his hands, running them under my shirt, and against my skin. With the skills that would make a magician proud, he unhooks my bra and releases my breasts. His hands continue moving, sliding between my breasts and the fabric until he finds my nipples and begins to gently massage. I sit up, giving him easier access.

"Shouldn't we be talking to Edon and figuring this new twist in our plotline out?"

"Later." He stands, picking me up with him. I pull my shirt and bra completely off on the way to the bed. He lays me down gently before taking his shirt off and lowering himself on top of me. His kisses are slow and precise as he takes one breast into his hand and the other into his mouth. Unlike this morning, he's taking his time, making sure to hit every spot along the way. My back arches as he reaches the perfect spot behind my ear. Warm kisses send shivers down my spine, and I want him inside of me now. My hips rise, touching him in response.

Reaching down, I unbutton his jeans and squeeze my hands through the waistband to his rock-hard ass. I squeeze his skin under my hands, and he moans in response. Working my way toward the zipper, I manage to pull his jeans down enough to expose his backside.

Topher sits up, pulling my leggings and underwear off in the process. Lying on a bed butt naked with my legs open would normally make me feel extremely self-conscious. With Topher, it feels unnaturally comfortable. "This is a little one-sided. I need your pants off now, sir."

He stands and slowly pulls his jeans off his body. Topher lowers himself on top of me, letting the hardest part of him touch the softest part of me. He finds my mouth and gently kisses, sending more chills than before. This morning was hot and passionate. Tonight is slow and full of emotion. He slowly lines himself up and fills me from the inside out. I gasp at the feeling.

"Are you okay?" His voice is low and sexy against my mouth.

"I'm more than okay." He begins to move slowly, making our connection even hotter than before. This is what making love is. Tears fill my eyes at the realization that until this moment, I've never made love.

I wrap my legs and arms around him, trying to pull him as close as possible. I want every inch of him in, on, and around me. It doesn't take long before we're both breathing hard. His mouth hasn't left mine as he continues moving in slow, deep thrusts. "Amelia," he whispers into my mouth at the same moment we both cry out. He buries himself one last time deep inside of me, and my entire body shudders at our connection.

We're both breathing harder than if we'd just gone for a run, as the aftermath of the best orgasm I've ever experienced in my life leaves my body. Topher slides out of me, pulling me to his side and holding me tightly. "That was amazing," he says between pants.

I wrap my leg around his and bury my head in his chest, craving intimacy. I've never felt so connected to a person before. From the other side of the room, my phone rings, drawing us back to reality. "Dammit," I pant.

"It might be something important."

I look up at the lycanthrope who just rocked my world. "Then they'll call back."

"Normally, I'd agree with you, but it could be Celeste."

Realizing he's right, I run naked across the brick floor to where my phone is sitting. I don't recognize the number on the caller ID. *"Hello?"*

"What's going on?" Celeste's voice says on the other end.

"Celeste?"

"I'm here. Are you okay?"

"I'm okay, but I won't be for long."

"What does that mean?"

I pause before answering. *"Hypatia changed the three months she originally gave Viktor to two weeks."*

"What are you talking about?"

"He didn't tell you?"

She sighs. *"No. He's been...distant since I returned."*

"Hypatia gave him three months to turn you in."

"Dammit. That explains why he insisted we leave the city."

"Where are you?" I ask.

"I think it's safer for you to not know."

"Celeste, she's going to kill me."

"No, she won't. I won't allow it."

"How do you expect to stop her when neither you nor Viktor is here?" Anger sounds through my voice.

"I have to go," her voice is soft. *"Don't worry. I'll figure something out. Call me at this number if you need me. I'll keep it near me."*

"Celeste? I don't know what to do."

"Trust your instincts." The line goes silent.

I pull the phone away, staring at the open line as Topher comes to my side. "What happened?"

"She hung up on me. I thought she'd be the one person to be there for me." Topher takes the phone away from me, setting it on the countertop. "I have no one."

He lifts my chin toward his. "That's not true. I'm not going anywhere. I'll be right here for as long as you need or want me." He wraps his arms around my back, pulling me into his chest. For the first time in a long time, I cry. Not a normal cry, but an ugly cry as the realization of my situation hits me like a lead brick.

Once the crying settles down, I tell Topher everything she said. "What do you think that means?"

"She said to trust your instincts. That's what we'll do."

"I'm going to take a shower." Outside, the streets are empty because of the torrential rainstorm that's taken over the city. I move to the bathroom, turning the water as hot as possible. The shower feels perfect but does little to relieve the tension of everything that's going on. Celeste said to trust my instincts, and right now, my instincts are telling me to get out of the city. But I can't do that because my lovely mother decided to rear her head years after abandoning me.

God, I miss my simple life of living in the closet without power. At least I knew what dangers were out there. All I had to do was get to school and back without being discovered, and I was good to go. Now, I have an ancient vampire organization out to kill me, a psychotic mother who's out to murder everyone in the city, a half-sister who can shift into a wolf, and a maker who has abandoned me when I need her the most.

I sulk in the shower long enough to use all the hot water. Exiting, I find a pair of fuzzy pajamas and a matching towel on the sink waiting for me, along with a fresh bottle of blood. Of all the things that are going wrong right now, Topher is the good. I take time drying off and getting dressed before finding him on the couch with his feet propped on the table in front of him.

I slide one leg over his and collapse into his lap. He wraps his arms around me protectively, holding me to his chest. "Thank you for my clothes and the blood."

"You're welcome." By the time I leave his lap, the water heater has had time to refill and give him the shower he deserves.

While Topher's in the shower, I order him two hamburgers and several side items to be delivered to the loft. The food shows up at the same time Topher exits the bathroom.

"What's that?"

"I cooked." I smile.

"God, that smells delicious. I'm starved." He sits at the bar, pulling the plate of food toward him. "You didn't have to order anything. I would've been okay."

"You took care of me. It's my turn to do the same."

He eats every bite in record time and even cleans up his plate afterward. "How about a movie?"

"Sure, but nothing epic tonight. I'm in the mood for something that doesn't require a lot of brain power."

"I know just the thing." He opens Netflix and pulls up an older movie that I've never seen.

The Proposal?

"Yep. It was Mom's favorite movie. She said it made her laugh even when she didn't feel like laughing." He pushes play, and I snuggle as close as possible to my personal heater and turn the world off, at least for a few hours.

Topher falls asleep after the movie. I tuck a blanket around him and head toward my Kindle for my nightly entertainment. A book I've never seen before pulls up on my suggested menu. The cover features a picture of a nearly naked human torso covered in muscular abs with a wolf head and claws, wrapped around a human woman wearing a bright red bikini and long, flowing blonde hair. "*My Wolfgasm Love,*" I read the title out loud. One glance at the lycanthrope asleep on my couch, and I know this will be my series for the night.

I finish the fourth and final book of the series just as the sun rises over the horizon. This series has given me serious trauma about lycan and the whole fated mate thing.

"What are you reading?" Topher's sleepy voice asks from the other end of the couch.

"I'm not sure you want to know."

"Sure, I do. Is it another vampire story?"

I laugh. "No, werewolves and their fated mates. It's

an entire series, based on different alphas and their mates.”

Topher sits up, wiping the sleep away from his eyes. “That sounds comedic.”

“I’m going with traumatic.” I close the cover on my Kindle. “Knotting.”

“What?”

“Knotting. Do lycanthrope really do that?”

He scratches his head. “Like dogs?” I don’t answer, just stare, waiting for an answer. “That sounds extremely painful and not a lot of fun. To answer your question, no, lycan don’t knot.” He cringes at the thought.

“Okay, good. I think I’m done reading fated mate series. That was a little much.”

“Sounds like a plan.” He laughs. “What is on the books for the day? No pun intended.”

I sigh. “We’re running out of time on Hypatia’s countdown.”

He moves next to me. “Let’s leave the city. Let’s pack up and leave this insanity behind. We can stay away from Hypatia and the council, stay one step ahead of them.” His large hand cups the side of my face, turning me to face him. “We can do it. We’re smarter than they are. We could hide in the bayou for a while then move around as needed.”

Tears immediately flow down my cheeks. I wrap my fingers around his large hand. “Topher, I love the fact that you’re willing to do that for me, but I can’t take you away from your family, from your future. You're going to be the next Alpha of New Orleans. Running away with a vampire isn't in your cards."

"Fuck the alpha thing. I don't care about being in charge anyway. I care about you."

I pull his palm away from my face, kissing it gently. "I care about you, too. You're the only solid thing in my life right now. I don't want to mess that up. Like it or not, your life was decided for you before you were born. There's no way in hell I'm going to come between you and fate."

"Amelia, I'm a grown man who makes his own choices. I choose you."

I stand, moving toward the window. "This isn't a choice you can make that easily. Hypatia will find us; she'll find me. Everything you will have given up for me will be for nothing. She will kill you without a second thought, and I'm not strong enough to protect you. You're not strong enough to protect you. I won't let that happen. I won't watch you die."

He's in front of me in an instant. My back pushed against the brick wall, his hands around my back protectively. "I will not let her harm you," Topher growls.

"Then we don't have a choice. We have to fight, but that fight needs to be here, in New Orleans. We're stronger here. We have support, little as it may be." His lips are on mine in a fit of passion. Claws rip my leggings into shreds as he throws them across the room. He pulls my legs around his hips and enters me without hesitation. Within seconds we're crying out in ecstasy, together. His eyes flash from their normal green color to bright red then back again.

"You're mine," he growls, kissing me deeper.

"I'm yours," I echo between kisses.

An hour later, the sexual tension between us has settled enough that I'm able to shower and get dressed for the day. I tell my expensive leggings goodbye as I throw them into the trash. Sometime yesterday, Topher restocked the blood supply in my refrigerator, and I'm grateful. I've had one already this morning and am working on number two. This hunger is getting out of control.

Topher and I decided the best way to get this party started is a meeting with Edon and Phillipe. I texted Phillipe not long ago and requested a meeting with the small group of vampire leaders in the city while Topher did the same with Edon. The only way we're going to be able to defeat this insanity is with the help of both groups.

the meeting

WE ARRIVE at LaLaurie Mansion not long after setting up the meeting place there. Edon and one of Topher's brothers are waiting at the front door. They're standing among a group of tourists on a ghost tour, pretending to be interested in the history of the home. I smirk at the irony.

"Amelia, this is my son, Zeke," Edon introduces the young lycanthrope as we approach them.

Zeke smiles and looks knowingly between his brother and me. "Shut up," Topher smirks as the four of us enter the home.

Phillipe, Erick, and Violet are in the back room, already sitting around the large conference table. They stand as we enter.

Violet takes her time looking the new wolf up and down with an approving smirk. Zeke looks uncomfortable immediately.

"Topher and I have something we need to share with you all." I take control of the meeting. "You are all aware of Hypatia and the council's threat to kill Celeste and...me."

I pause before continuing. "Edon, Topher, and I have become aware of another threat that affects more than the two of us." I take a deep breath before continuing. "My mother, Tammy, is still alive."

Erick stands from the table. "Please don't think this crude, dear girl, but how does that affect both of our communities?"

"Because she's the one responsible for the attacks on the lycan bar and the death of Brian," I answer.

"How is that possible?" Violet asks. "She's human." She looks across the table at the lycan Alpha. "Isn't she?"

"She's half-human," I answer. "Her mother was, is a lycanthrope."

Phillipe rocks his seat backward. "A hybrid?"

"Yes," Edon speaks for the first time.

"What does that mean?" Violet asks.

"It means she's stronger than a full-blooded lycan," he answers.

"Please share with me how that's possible." Erick sits back in his leather office chair. "How is a hybrid stronger than someone with full blood?"

"To be honest, not a lot is known about hybrids. Until Tammy, we weren't aware of any that have survived until adulthood, let alone, lived long enough to have children."

"Tammy was able to slice Brian's head cleanly off without any evidence of a struggle on Brian's part. She was able to orchestrate the attack on both our groups. She's strong and crazy. That's a lethal combination." Topher takes control of the meeting. For the first time since I've known him, he acts like the alpha he's trained to be.

"What are you suggesting?" Phillipe asks.

I stand, moving next to Topher. "Tammy plans on killing anyone who caused her pain in her past. In her mind, that's any and all lycan and vampire alive in the city."

Erick laughs. "She's one hybrid woman. What could she possibly do to destroy every wolf and vampire in the city?"

"Tammy's not going to stop with destroying the mythological creatures of New Orleans. She doesn't care who she hurts. Humans are not excluded," I answer.

"She has the power to shift into wolf form, exposing our kind to the humans around us," Topher adds.

"No offense, young man, but what does that have to do with the vampire community?" Erick is persistent.

"Because if lycan exists, it will only be a matter of time until we're discovered," Violet answers. "Humans are nothing but curious."

"Would it be so bad if we were discovered?" Zeke speaks for the first time.

"Yes," the room answers in unison.

"Humans are not ready for the truth," Phillipe continues.

"You think Tammy is more of a threat than Hypatia?" Violet stands, stepping away from the table.

"Hypatia is here for me and Celeste, who is missing. In the grand scheme of things, yes. I'm one person. The city of New Orleans has hundreds of thousands of people. The odds are pretty obvious." I feel the heat coming from Topher at my words.

"Why don't we let Hypatia take care of her?" Violet asks. "I mean think about it. Hypatia and the council's entire job is keeping the vampire community in control and out of human consciousness. If Tammy is threatening to expose both communities, let them do their job. Let them take her down."

I scoff at the idea. "Violet, that's easier said than done."

"Why?" she asks. "Let the two problems take care of themselves."

Topher looks at me with a smirk. "It might just work."

"How?" I ask the group.

Violet claps her hands loudly. "A ball!"

"Violet, this isn't the twentieth century. Balls aren't a thing anymore," Erick answers.

Topher crosses his arms over his chest before speaking. "No. She could be onto something. We could promote it through both communities. Tammy's connected somehow, or she wouldn't have known which locations to attack. We make a huge deal out of it and invite the council, claiming the ball is in their honor. Tammy's not going to miss an opportunity to destroy that many vampires and lycan at one time."

"You can't be seriously considering this?" Erick asks, looking around the room.

"We can," Phillipe answers.

Erick stands to argue, and I'm seriously reconsidering the time I saved his life. "Has anyone considered the fact that it may not be that easy? What if the council refuses to come? What if Tammy doesn't show up, and we've just handed them Amelia on a silver platter? None of us are strong enough to save her if it comes to that." He turns to me, looking me in the eyes. "Are you prepared to sacrifice yourself in that case?"

I take a deep breath, ready to answer when Topher answers for me. "We will not allow that to happen. *I* will not allow that to happen."

"Dear boy, puppy love is one thing, but fighting the oldest vampire in existence is another. You will not win. Your father will not win. Hypatia will not be alone, she will be surrounded by others nearly as old as she is. I understand your connection to Amelia. Hell, we can smell you all over her, but love isn't enough to win a fight."

"It's a risk I'm willing to take," I answer softly.

"Hypatia and the council will kill me either way. Whether they're able to kill Tammy will have nothing to do with my survival. I'd rather go out fighting for the ones I care about and the city I care about than sit back and wait for them to show up at my doorstep." Topher laces his fingers through mine, kissing the back of my hand.

"Do you realize what you're asking?" Phillipe joins.

"I do," I answer truthfully. "I'm asking you to use me for the good of the city and our communities." Topher's grip on my fingers gets tighter.

Phillipe looks me in the eyes, making his decision. "Where will the ball be held?" he asks, several minutes later.

"Leave that to me!" Violet jumps to her feet, ready to plan the event of a lifetime. "I'll get to work on it immediately."

"We're running out of time," I remind her. "It has to be this weekend."

"Amelia, the weekend is in three days. Do you know what you're asking?" Violet asks.

I smile weakly. "If anyone can do it, you can."

"Oh, you're right." She stands, taking her designer bag with her. "I'll be in touch by the end of the day with the details." She touches Zeke's butt on her way out the door. He jumps at her touch but smiles a wicked grin.

"Amelia, are you sure about this?" Erick asks again.

"Yes."

He stands, moving to my side. "I will protect you

any way I can." He wraps his arms around me, hugging me. "I will never forget you saved my life. I will return the favor if I can."

"Thank you." I return the hug.

Phillipe moves next to us. "The same for me." He squeezes my shoulder.

"Thank you, Phillipe." I watch the two vampires exit the front door of the mansion.

"I will get the word out to our community. I don't know how many will be willing to mingle with vampires, but enough will come to make it appealing to Tammy." Edon moves to my side. "You know we will protect you with our lives, right?"

"I do, but I won't allow that to happen." I look between the three giant lycan in front of me. "You have to promise me that you won't sacrifice yourselves for me."

"You can't be serious," Topher says.

"Promise me, or I will do this on my own, without the help of your community."

Edon and Zeke lower their heads. "I promise," each man responds separately.

"Are you fucking kidding me?" Topher slams his father into the wall behind him. "You promised Mom that you would protect Amelia with your life. Now that the opportunity comes for you to stand up to that promise and be a man, you renounce it? What the hell, Dad?"

"Topher, I..."

"No, I don't want to hear anything you have to say. Amelia, I'll be out front." He turns, storming out of the mansion.

"Edon, I'm sorry." I help him stand from the lycanthrope-sized indention he made in the wall behind him.

"Don't apologize. He has every right to be angry. I will do everything in my power to keep from putting you in danger. My wife died protecting you. I refuse to let her sacrifice be in vain."

"I don't plan on it getting to that point either." I follow them out of the mansion and find Topher sitting on a bench across the street.

"Good luck with that one," Zeke says, nodding toward his older brother.

I move to the bench, sitting next to the pissed-off wolf and nudging him on the shoulder. "You, okay?"

"No," he answers.

"I'm going to be okay," I whisper.

He turns, facing me. "How can you be so sure?"

"Because I have everything to live for." I lean my head against his chest as he wraps his arm around me.

The morning passes relatively quickly, and neither of us brings the subject up again. We've stayed in the Quarter, visiting antique stores and small family-owned businesses for most of the afternoon until the stomach rumbling coming from both of us becomes more than either of us can bear. "You need to eat," he announces after my latest rumbles.

"Let's get something for you, and we can head back to my loft for mine."

"It's a plan." He wraps his arm around my shoulder as we head toward a small restaurant on Royal Street.

"Aren't you two cute?" a female voice says behind us.

I turn, knowing who it is without looking. "Hello, Tammy."

"A wolf and a vampire, together in public. That's something I thought I'd never see."

I look around, hoping no humans were in earshot of her words. "What do you want?" I ask.

"I told you I'd be in touch."

"That you did. To what do we owe the honor?"

"Can't a mother visit her daughter?"

"No. What do you want?" I spew.

Tammy sighs. "Oh, alright. You've dragged it out of me." She holds her hand up, showing me a detonator button.

"What is that?"

"What does it look like?" She smirks. "I'm thinking that house you were meeting in earlier could use a facelift."

Oh, my God. I move vampire speed in front of my mother, reaching for the detonator before she can push the button. She moves faster than me, sliding out of my reach and to the other side of the street. "Is this what you're after?"

"No!" I scream. "You'll kill hundreds of innocent people in the process."

"Innocent people? What did those innocent people do to protect me?"

"Protect you from what? You're the one who killed your foster father. Why would you need protection?"

"Say goodbye, Amelia." She raises her thumb dramatically just as a giant dark brown wolf appears out of nowhere, knocking her to the ground and the detonator a few feet in front of her.

Tammy shifts from the familiar image of my mother to a wolf equal in size to the one in front of her. She snarls, as groups of humans stop in the middle of the street with their phones pointed at the duo. "Shit!" I yell. Running toward the ensuing fight, I grab the detonator, breaking it in half and destroying the electronics inside.

I move vampire speed to every human gawking, knocking their phones to the ground and smashing them before they realize what's happened. Behind me, the wolves circle each other and are moments away from a fight. I step between them. "No, Tammy. This is not the answer. If you hurt him, I will kill you." My body shudders and instead of the non-scary teeth that usually make their appearance, I turn into a creature similar to Celeste when she fought off the strigoi. "You will not survive." Topher moves to my side, snarling. The human audience has abandoned their shattered phones and moved to safety.

Tammy shivers, turning back into the familiar image of my mother. "This isn't over," she growls, moving away from our fight. Topher shakes his head, and in an instant, he's standing in front of me in human form without any clothes on. Whatever caused me to change into the gargoyle-looking creature leaves, and I'm transformed back into the short red-haired version of myself.

Topher looks down. "This is going to be hard to explain." The groups of humans come out of hiding and back into the streets. A young woman starts clapping and before long the rest of the group joins her. "What the hell?" he whispers.

"This is New Orleans. In any other city, it would be weird. Not here." I wave at our audience and bow dramatically. "Thank you, ladies and gentlemen. Catch the rest of our show tonight, on Bourbon Street."

Topher covers his package with his hands, and I keep watch on the backside as we head toward my loft. Thankfully, we are in a city where this sort of thing happens regularly, and not many people notice or pay attention to us. "I'm enjoying the view," I tease from behind.

"Not helping." We get to my apartment, and he enters the code, separating us from the insanity of our lives. My phone buzzes as soon as we're up the spiral staircase.

You are cordially invited to the coming-out ball for Miss Violet Du Four.

This Friday at 8:00 pm. The location will be delivered one hour prior.

"Looks like we need to go shopping."

shopping with a lycan

TOPHER WALKS out of the bathroom, wearing a pair of perfectly fitted jeans, a black T-shirt, and a belt. Through the tight-fitted shirt, I can see every muscle that covers his stomach. "I'm a fan of you naked, but this is a close second."

He saunters his way toward me, smirking the entire trip. "Thank you, ma'am." He uses his Southern Gentlemen voice as he slides next to me on the bar. "I'm still hungry. Did you eat?"

"I did. While you were getting dressed, I drank two bottles."

"What happened back there?" he asks the question I had hoped to avoid.

"Tammy lost her shit."

"You know what I mean. What happened to you? Has something like that happened before?"

I find an off-colored fleck in the quartz countertop

and rub my fingers across it subconsciously. "No. That was a first."

"I've never seen a vampire do that before. Hell, I've never seen a vampire do anything except sit around and drive expensive cars. What was that?"

I shrug. "I don't know. I've seen Celeste turn into the same thing but never had it happen to me."

"Do you think because she's your maker, it's something you picked up from her?"

"I don't know. The person who might know isn't around to ask, so I'm taking this one day at a time." I stand, hoping to escape the conversation. "Let's go grab you some food and do some shopping. I don't have anything appropriate for a ball, especially one that Violet's in charge of."

Thankfully, Topher doesn't push the issue and follows me out of the loft. We drive toward the only place I know that might have formal wear in stock—the mall. We pull my BMW into the parking garage and head straight to the food court. Every person we pass looks at Topher. Old, young, male, female, it doesn't matter. They all stop and stare. He wraps his arm around my shoulder, oblivious to the attention he's receiving.

He orders two large pizzas and eats both of them in record time. "You were hungry."

"I told you. I'm a growing boy." My stomach growls, interrupting his words.

"Dammit," I whisper at the sound. "How can I still be hungry?"

"Maybe because of what happened today."

"That makes sense." I stand, grabbing my bag. "Let's do some shopping. Distraction will help."

We move to the first store that looks like they carry what we're looking for. "Can I help you?" an older man greets us as we enter.

"We're looking for in stock formal wear."

"Of course, follow me." He leads us across the store to a corner filled with sequins and sparkles. "Please take your time looking, and we will check back on you momentarily."

"This is fancier than any place I've ever been," Topher whispers as the man walks away.

"Yeah, I didn't grow up shopping at places like this either." I move to a dark green dress, covered in sequins.

"That would look beautiful on you," my personal cheerleader says from behind. He moves to a shorter version in black, pulling one off the rack, along with a silver tea-length dress with a fuller skirt. "This is fun."

Topher sits on the bench outside of the dressing room, as the attendant goes into the room with me. I try the dresses on in order of least favorite to most favorite, starting with the tea-length silver.

He whistles loudly, embarrassing me as I model the dress for him. "I like that one. It's my favorite so far."

"It's not too short for a ball?"

"You are asking the wrong person for that." He smiles. "Go show me more."

I come back, wearing the knee-length black sequin dress, and Topher's pupils enlarge. "Damn, I like that one even more."

I stand in the middle of the three-fold mirror, looking at the dress from all sides. "I love it, but I think it might be too short. Let me go try on the last one."

In the mirror, I see a smirk cover his face. The attendant helps me zip the skin-tight green dress that is the perfect length for my short legs. On an average-sized woman, it would be tea-length. On me, it's the perfect length for a pair of heels. The green sequins sparkle against my red hair, and I fall in love instantly.

Topher stands as soon as I exit the dressing room. He stares at me speechless. "You don't need to say anything. I can tell you like it." I smile.

"Like it? God, you look...stunning. Please tell me this is the one we're buying."

"This is the one we're buying," I echo.

He's on me in an instant, his arms wrapped around my waist. "Can I help take it off?" he whispers for my ears only. The heat rises in my cheeks and other places.

I clear my throat and step away. "No, we have more shopping to do. I need shoes, a bag, jewelry, and you need a tux."

"I'll just wear jeans."

"I'm a fan of you in jeans, but no. I want to see you in a tux."

He steps away as the young attendant comes to my side. "Is this the one, Miss Lockhart?"

"It is, thank you." She follows me back into the dressing room and helps me unzip the dress.

"I'll have it out front for you when you're ready. If there's anything else you'd like to purchase, we can add them to the dress, and you'll only have to cash out once."

I exit, finding Topher leaning against the wall with his eyes closed. "Tired?" I ask, just as my stomach growls again.

"No. I'm just holding the image of you in that dress tightly in my mind." He stands, pulling me toward the dressing room. The attendant is busy and doesn't notice us sneaking inside. He leads me to the back and sits down on the empty chair. "Drink from me. I know you're hungry."

"Topher, I'm not going to do that in a dressing room."

"Do you have a better idea? Want me to ask the attendant if she's willing to volunteer?" My stomach growls, betraying me once again. He sticks his wrist in front of me. "Drink. I'll heal before we even leave this room."

I pull his wrist toward me and focus on not making it painful. "If at any time I hurt you, pull away immediately." He nods, keeping his arm in place.

I sink my teeth into his wrist, and the warmth that floods my mouth is exactly what I need. Topher lowers to his knees, making us close to the same height. As I feed off him, he kisses my neck and exposed shoulders. The combination of the warm kisses and his blood nearly brings me to an orgasm in the middle of the store. I come to reality and withdraw my teeth from his wrist, licking the wounds. They seal before my eyes. Topher pulls away from my neck, his pupils are dilated and the look on his face mirrors mine.

"Do you know how bad I want you right now?"

"Do you know how tempted I am to let you?"

"Mrs. Lockhart? Are you in here?" The attendant comes back into the dressing room.

I clear my throat. "Yes, I forgot my bag." I stand, exiting the room with Topher on my heels.

"Oh," the attendant exclaims as she tries to figure out what's going on.

"Thank you for your help." He smiles at the confused girl.

Topher follows me to the shoe department, holding both of my hands as we walk. He moves toward a pair of three-inch stripper heels and a long string that ties around the ankles. "These are kind of cool."

"If you want to witness me break my ankles as I walk, those are perfect."

"Well, at least you'd heal quickly." He sets the shoe down, moving to a much more sensible version with silver rhinestones and buckle closure. "What about these?"

"Those are actually nice." The older man who began

following us the instant we entered the shoe department comes out of the back room, carrying a pair in my size. He sits in front of me, helping me out of my dirty Converse high tops, and slides the sequin sandal on my foot.

"This fits you quite well, Miss Lockhart. Shall I wrap it up?"

"Yes, thank you. We have a few more things to look at before completing our shopping."

"Of course. Let me know if I may be of any more service."

Topher follows me out of the shoe department as we head toward the men's department. "These people are friendlier than where I usually shop."

"Yeah, Walmart isn't much on customer service."

Topher bellows out a laugh. "That would be offensive if it weren't true."

An emerald green tuxedo, the same color as my dress, catches my attention immediately. "This would look amazing with your eyes."

"You think so?"

"I know so."

He pulls it off the rack and looks at the price tag before hanging it back on the rack. "We need to stick with Walmart."

I pull it back off and send him toward the dressing room. "I have money, and I'm not taking no for an answer. This will be courtesy of Viktor."

"In that case." He laughs, heading into the dressing room.

He returns a few minutes later, and my suspicions are confirmed. The tuxedo is the perfect match for his eyes and fits him like it was made for him. "That is perfect," I say as he comes toward me.

"You don't think the pants are too tight?" He turns, showing me his ass.

"Absolutely not. They're perfect."

"I'm just a piece of meat to you, aren't I?"

I pat him on the butt, and he hurries back to the dressing room. "Hang it up. We're taking it."

Our last stop is the jewelry department where I let Topher choose the earrings and necklace. He chooses the perfect color and a matching arm cuff. We head back over to where the young girl is holding my dress and pay for the items.

Topher clears his throat when he sees the total appear on the register screen. I hand her the credit card Viktor gave me before we left for Haiti, and it's accepted without any issue. "That was fun," he announces on the way back to the car. "I enjoyed spending Viktor's money."

"It was worth it to see you in that tux again."

"I'd say the same for that dress."

Topher carries our purchases up to the loft, hanging his tux next to my dress. The colors match perfectly. I ask him a question that's plagued me since the fight this morning. "Topher?"

"Hmm?" He lays down beside me on the bed.

"When Tammy changed into wolf form, did she look different than normal?"

He crosses his legs at the ankles. "To be honest, I didn't have much time to look. I did notice she was larger than our females. She was almost the same size I was."

"Aren't you bigger because you're the future alpha?"

"Yes. I've never seen a female that big."

I turn, facing him. "Could it have something to do with her being a hybrid?"

"I don't know. Until Tammy, I never knew there were such things."

"That was the first time I've seen you shift." My voice is no louder than a whisper. I tilt my head, looking him in the eyes. "Your eyes were the same. You were beautiful."

Topher laughs and pulls me closer. "I'd prefer terrifying, but I'll take beautiful."

"Do you think this is going to work? Do you think the council will take out Tammy?" It feels strange asking if someone will kill my mother. If I'm honest with myself, she's never been a mother to me or poor little Becky, for that matter.

"I do. I don't think she stands a chance against them."

"What about me?"

"I think I will fight until the death to make sure nothing happens to you."

I fight the tears threatening to fall. "That's what I'm afraid of."

He lifts my chin, pulling my lips to his. "It's not too late to leave. We could be across the world by the time of the ball. Putting you in that situation pisses me the hell off."

"I know. Thank you for trusting me." I pull my legs in front of me, curling into Topher's arms. His breathing slows down and becomes more rhythmic as he drifts off to sleep, leaving me alone with my thoughts.

preparing for who knows what

INSTEAD OF FATED MATES, tonight I choose something more dignified to read—dragon shifters. I finish the last book of the series just as the sun rises. Sliding off the bed, I slip into the shower before Topher wakes up. It's Thursday morning, which means the ball is tomorrow night. One more day before the council chooses to leave me alone and kill Tammy or kill both of us.

I take my time, enjoying the hot water. The shower door opens, and Topher walks in without a word. He slides behind me, wrapping his arms around the front of my body and grabbing a breast in each hand. Warm lips lower to my earlobe, then move even further to my neck. One of his hands continues lower, over my belly button, and down to the part of me that's already throbbing for his touch.

"Topher," I whisper.

"Shh," he responds, inches from my ear. His fingers gently rub in circles, opening me enough for his hand to move exactly where I want it. His touch takes my breath away as he begins his slow and precise assault. My body melts into his hands.

"Tell me what you want," he growls.

"I...I," I pant. "I want you inside of me." He bends me over without another word and enters me from behind, filling me completely. I brace my hands against the tile wall, opening my legs wide to give him access. He moves in rhythm with his hand, slowly rubbing in just the right spot.

Topher begins breathing hard as he props his free arm against the tile in front of us. Between the slow circles of his hand and the fullness of him inside me, I cry out in pleasure just as he does the same. It takes all my strength to remain standing. I turn, facing him, and kiss him with all the emotion building inside me. "Amelia," he whispers.

"I know," I answer. "Don't say anything you're going to regret."

"I'd never regret anything with you." He picks me up, carrying me to the bed where we make love until both of our stomachs are growling louder than our orgasms.

"We both need to eat," I announce moving toward the refrigerator. I come back with bottles of blood and orange juice before climbing back into bed.

"This is the best way to spend the day," he says,

setting his empty bottle on the nightstand beside the bed. My phone buzzes from the other side of the bed.

> The council has accepted our invitation. Hypatia, along with the four other members, will be in attendance.

I read the text out loud to Topher who doesn't respond. Instead, he wraps his arms around me, pulling me close. "Let's watch a movie. We don't have anything more important to do, and I want to spend every minute I can with you."

"Before…"

"No," he interrupts. "Don't add any more to that sentence." We dress in matching sweat clothes and relocate from the bed to the couch. With everything that's going on, I find it impossible to focus on anything other than the ball tomorrow.

By the time the sun is setting, Topher's stomach growls are out of control. Neither one of us wants to leave, and he decides to call for food delivery. An hour later a woman delivers three bags full of his favorite delicacies, and he eats every bite.

Somehow the sun is rising, and I have no recollection of how we got here. Did I just waste the last night I might have with Topher? Netflix is playing the second season of a series, and I have no idea what's happened throughout the first. Topher's long body is stretched on the couch beside me, with his head on my lap. Soft snores warm my heart.

His shoulder-length hair is out of its usual bun and lays around his head in a beautiful spray that's fitting for a hair commercial. I take a minute, admiring his features. He's beautiful, so warm, so alive. There's no doubt Topher will risk his life for mine tonight if it comes down to that. I refuse to let that happen.

"Did I fall asleep?" his sleepy voice asks from my lap.

"You did." I smile. "It's Friday."

He sits up, rubbing his hands through his already crazy hair. "What's on the docket for the day?"

"I want to have my hair and makeup professionally done. I don't want to look like the Walmart version of Amelia tonight." He laughs at my choice of words. "I'm going to ask Violet to go with me. She has connections."

"Okay. While you're doing that, I'll check in with Edon."

I pick up my phone, sending a quick text to Violet with my request. She responds within minutes, and we make plans to meet at our usual salon at noon.

The morning passes quickly, and before I realize it, it's time to meet Violet. I walk into the salon to find a familiar face. "Ollie?" I rush to the tall vampire standing next to Violet.

He wraps his arms around me, lifting me off the ground. "I've missed you, Amelia."

It seems like a lifetime ago since I've seen the blonde English professor vampire. "Where have you been?"

He smiles, moving back to Violet's side. "I returned to Mississippi after we took care of the cult leader. I've been back and forth a few times since. Violet kept me up-to-date on everything that's happened here. I'm sorry about Viktor and Celeste."

I shrug, and for the first time, I realize I don't care. "Are you coming to the ball tonight?"

"I wouldn't miss it." He bends down, kissing Violet on the forehead. "While you ladies get prepared in here, I'm going to run a few errands." He gives me a side hug on the way out of the door. "I'll see you tonight."

Violet claps her hands as only Violet can. "Ready? I reserved the salon for the rest of the day."

We turn and the host of hairdressers jumps to attention. We spend the next four hours being pampered from head to toe. It's been a few years since I've had a pedicure, and I'm embarrassed for the poor woman who has to perform the service. I show Violet a picture of the dress I purchased and let her decide which hairstyle and makeup will match the best. The final product is anything except Walmart Amelia.

"You look beautiful," Violet says from her chair. She looks as beautiful as always.

"Thank you. So do you."

I hand Viktor's credit card to the woman at the register without blinking an eye. "Everything is going to be okay, you know that, right?"

"No, I don't," I answer truthfully. "I don't think Hypatia or the council is going to be satisfied with a slap on the wrist. Without Celeste in grown-up form or Viktor here to swoon her, I don't know what's going to happen. Throw in the insanity of Tammy Sue, and we're in for a real shit show tonight."

"Tammy won't be any concern after tonight. I have no doubt the council will take care of her." She wraps her arm through mine on the way to our cars. "No one would blame you if you don't show up. You and that hot wolf you're banging could get out of here. There's still time."

"I know, and believe me, I've thought about it. But I have to see this thing through. No matter how far I run or where I go, they'll find me. I can't do that to Topher. I can't do that to myself. I won't spend the rest of my life on the run."

Violet pulls me tight. "I'm so proud of you. You're not that scared little girl that Harrison dragged into his home anymore."

I scoff. "Now I'm a scared vampire who doesn't know what the hell she's doing."

"I'll see you tonight." She hands me a piece of paper with the address of the ball listed.

I wait for her to pull out before starting my car and heading back to the loft. The address is in the warehouse district, which is not a surprise. Knowing Violet, it will look like she's spent months preparing. By the time I park and get inside, there are only a few hours remaining before it's time to get ready. Topher's in the kitchen, eating a large meal he ordered from some-where. He freezes in place as I enter.

"You look beautiful." He moves quickly to my side, gently touching the ends of my curls. "You're always beautiful, but damn."

"Thank you." I head to the refrigerator, grabbing a bottle of blood my stomach craves. "How was Edon?"

"His normal chipper self. They've done everything they can to make sure Tammy knows about the ball without sending her an outright invitation."

"She'll be there." I finish the blood, throwing the bottle in the recycle bin. "She's not going to miss an opportunity to kill that many vampires and lycan in the same location." Why am I talking about this like it's nothing? Has my life changed so much in a year that this is my norm? "Violet gave me the address."

"Yeah, Edon had it already. He's been in contact with Violet, helping to get all of this organized. He looked more tired than usual. This has been hard on him." He sits back and finishes his meal. "I told Dad we'd be there around seven to help run a final security check on the building."

"Why are we securing the location? We want Tammy to show up."

"We don't know what she's going to do. I'd rather her show up in person, not plant a bomb in the building somewhere. A last-minute check is the only way to ensure that doesn't happen."

"That makes sense. I can be ready." I move to the

closet that holds the beautiful sequin dress. Neither of us says anything else as we dress in our matching green. The energy between us is heavy, both of us realizing what tonight could mean.

Topher zips the dress, helping me get everything in place. We stand in front of the large mirror leaning against the brick wall, staring at the fancy versions of ourselves. "We clean up pretty well." He tries to lighten the mood.

His hair is loose, hanging neatly to his shoulders and ending with small curls. The green tuxedo makes his eyes pop, and I realize just how beautiful he truly is. Taking both of his hands into mine, I turn, facing him. "Topher, no matter what happens tonight, I want you to know that these past few weeks have been the happiest of my life. Despite the impending doom and death threats, you are the best thing that's ever happened to me. I'm grateful to you for your protection, among other things."

"If we weren't so dressed up, I'd have a hard time not making love to you right now," he answers. "These two weeks have been the same for me. We're going to get out of this alive, both of us." His large hand cups my cheek. "You are the best thing that's ever happened to me. You make me a better man, a better son, and a better future alpha." He pauses. "I love you, Amelia. I know we haven't known each other long, but I've known I loved you since Jamaica. I knew it the moment I saw you. You're the one I'm meant to be with."

Tears fill my eyes. "I love you, too, Christopher St. James."

"When this is all over, we're going somewhere, just the two of us. Somewhere we can make love all day and walk around naked all night."

I laugh. "It's a plan."

"Until then, we have to put on the performance of a lifetime tonight."

I link my fingers through his. "Topher, promise me you won't sacrifice yourself for me."

"I won't make that promise."

"You will, and you will mean it."

He looks away. "How can you ask me to do that?"

"Because you're the future Alpha of New Orleans. That's more important than saving me from my psychotic mother or ancient vampires."

"How is that different?"

"Because you're important. You're special."

"You're important and special to me. Don't ask me to not fight for you," he retorts.

I look at our joined hands. I have no intention of putting him in that predicament. "Okay," I lie.

We pull into the valet stand at the warehouse as the clock on the dash flashes seven. A young man steps toward Topher's Mustang with a huge smile on his face. "This is sick, man."

"Thanks." Topher tosses him the keys. "Take care of her."

"Ready?" he asks, wrapping my arm through his.

"Nope." We enter the warehouse anyway.

the party of a lifetime

THE DECORATIONS ARE MORE than I imagined. Violet has a gift for making something beautiful out of nothing. I laugh at the irony of that thought, remembering our first trip to the mall.

Round tables are scattered throughout the floor. Each one holds enough place settings for eight, along with flower arrangements that stand at least two feet high. The bright red roses are the perfect contrast to the stark white tablecloths. Plus, what else screams vampire council of death better than red roses?

"Amelia!" Violet runs across the concrete floor in three-inch heels. Her dress is the same shade of purple as her hair. She looks like a runway model. She pulls me into a hug and notices mine and Topher's matching green. "You two look gorgeous!"

"You outdid yourself." I motion to the perfectly decorated space. "This is spectacular."

"Miss Du Four," a voice calls from the other side of the room.

"Thank you. I'll be back." She rushes toward the voice.

"I'm going to find Edon and help do a last-minute building sweep. Want to come with me?"

"No, I'll be good here. The guests shouldn't start arriving until closer to eight. I'll see if Violet needs any help before then."

He brings my hand to his lips, kissing it seductively and sending shivers down my spine. I watch his ass as he walks out of the building. It's a view I quite enjoy. Violet is across the room, directing two workers who are hanging up a large banner. "How hard is it to hang up a banner?" she whispers as I step to her side.

"Apparently, harder than it looks." My answer makes her giggle. "Can I help you do anything?"

"That would be great. Can you check on the caterers? They're in the kitchen. Just make sure they're ready to serve our meal at eight."

I leave her and find the caterers running around in the kitchen. The meal is just as you would suspect with a clientele of vampires and wolves. Half of the group is working on preparing what looks like steak tartare, while the others are filling glasses with blood.

"Can I help you, ma'am?" an older man wearing a tall hat asks as he rushes past me.

"Miss Du Four asked me to come and check on

everything and make sure you're going to be ready at eight."

"Yes, ma'am. Despite how chaotic it looks in here, we're right on schedule."

"I'll let her know." I step back as a tray of wine glasses full of red liquid passes by. My stomach growls at the smell.

Without another word, I exit the busy space and move toward the tables that line the front of the room. These are no doubt for our guests of honor, the council. Violet has name cards on each plate. Hypatia is front and center with two people on each side of her. On the other table lining the front, Edon's name is right in the middle. Topher and I have cards to his right side, while Zeke and someone named Jonathan sit on his left. Dammit, Violet. I don't want to be in front of everyone tonight.

"How are the caterers?" Violet asks, pulling me out of my head.

"They said everything was perfect." I turn toward the spot with my name. "Are you sure this is the best place for me to sit?"

"Yes," she answers, looking at her watch. "Shit, it's seven-thirty. The guests should begin arriving soon. Where's that wolf of yours?"

"Checking out the perimeter."

Violet laughs. "That perimeter has been checked out more times than I can count. Are you ready for this?"

"No," I answer truthfully. "I don't know what is going to happen."

"Yeah, me either, but I have a good feeling about it. Everything is going to work out in our favor." She gives me a quick hug.

"Thank you for doing all of this."

"Are you kidding? It's what I live for!" She scurries away, running like a track star in heels I would barely be able to walk in. She's right, guests begin arriving not long after, greeted by several humans dressed in the same style clothes as the guests. They direct the guests to their assigned seats, offering a welcoming smile. I wonder if they realize how close they might come to becoming dinner.

"Everything looks good outside," a familiar deep voice says behind me. Topher moves to my back and wraps his hands around my waist. "Everything good inside?"

"Yep. Dinner is ready to be served, and the guests are arriving. Violet outdid herself."

Topher leads me to the dance floor in front of a stage and a small jazz ensemble who've been playing since the guests began filling the room. "May I have this dance?"

"I'd be honored." We step to the middle of the dance floor as Topher wraps one hand around my waist and the other laced through mine. Other couples join us as we sway to the slow beat.

"Have I told you how beautiful you look tonight?"

"Yes, several times, but that doesn't mean you have to stop." I keep an eye on the door, waiting for a familiar and annoying ancient vampire to enter. Her bright pink hair will probably reflect off the décor, blinding half the room.

"Dad assured me that he made every effort to make sure Tammy knew about this tonight. I don't doubt she'll show up."

"Let's hope she doesn't decide to show up wearing a bomb vest."

He laughs. "She won't risk injury to herself."

"May I have this dance?" a deep voice says behind me. Topher's face changes in an instant. I turn, seeing the face that matches the voice I recognized. Viktor.

I look past him, searching for my maker. "Where's Celeste?"

"Dance?" he repeats, holding his hand toward me.

Topher growls low and deep as he moves between the two of us. "Topher," I whisper. "It's okay." I step toward Viktor and lay my hand on top of his. He leads us away from Topher to the other corner of the dance floor. Without a word, he wraps one hand around my waist, pulling me toward him.

"What the hell is this monstrosity?" he whispers.

"It's just what you think it is. A ball."

Viktor laughs, flashing his fangs. Why the hell are his fangs out?

"Why are you here, Viktor?"

"I was invited." He smiles, twirling me under his arm.

"That must have been an accident. I'll have to ask Violet about that."

"You look beautiful."

"You don't get to tell me that. In case you don't remember, you left me to fend for myself in another country and didn't give a shit about it."

"From the looks of you and that color-coordinated lycanthrope glaring at me right now, you did quite well in that country. His smell is all over you." He tries to twirl me again, and I refuse to move.

"Where did you go?"

"I took Celeste somewhere where she'd be safe."

"Yet, here you are, right back in the lion's den."

He looks at the wooden dance floor. "Celeste insisted."

"I knew she was here. Where is she?"

"Hiding," he whispers. "The council cannot know she's in the city." He pulls me closer until no space separates the two of us. "For what it's worth, I'm sorry. Celeste's life was more important."

"For what it's worth, I understand." My stomach growls, begging for more blood.

"Hungry, my dear?"

"Ladies and gentlemen," Violet's voice interrupts the music. "It seems our guests of honor have arrived." The crowd erupts into applause. "Please find your seat and prepare for our meal. Don't worry." She laughs. "I have arranged for the perfect meal for both of our communities."

"Why are you doing this?" Viktor asks. "What is the purpose of this show?"

"Maybe if you'd stayed in town, you'd know. Leave me the hell alone, and don't come near me anymore tonight. I don't want anything to do with you."

A hand wrapped around my wrist stops my escape. "You smell different," Viktor says, turning me toward him.

"Probably the wolf you smell all over me." My voice is full of sarcasm.

"No, it's you. *You* smell different."

"Whatever, Viktor. Leave me alone." I pull away from his grip, moving back toward Topher.

"Are you alright?" Topher asks, still glaring at the ancient vampire on the dance floor.

"I'm fine." I plaster on a fake smile. "Are you ready to get this party started?"

"I thought it was already started." He follows me to the main tables at the front of the room. We arrive at the tables at the same time as the council.

"Alexia! It's so good to see you again." She looks past me, assessing the lycanthrope behind me. "Who's this gorgeous wolf behind you?"

Hypatia moves past me to Topher. Her bright pink hair is even brighter than the last time I saw her, and the silver sequin dress she's wearing is the perfect contrast to the hue. "Christopher St. James," he says, holding his hand toward her. "It's a pleasure to meet you."

She smiles, moving closer to him. "Not as much as it is to meet you."

"Hypatia? Are you not going to introduce me to this lovely vampire?" An older man says, coming to my side.

"Leonard, this is Amy. She's the one you're here to meet."

I hold my hand out to his. "Amelia."

Leonard is wearing a tuxedo with tails that look straight out of the thirteen hundreds. His long white hair is pulled back into a low ponytail, and his dark brown eyes take in every inch of me. "You're much lovelier than I had you pictured."

"Thank you?"

Topher leads me away from the council and to our seats at the table. Edon and Zeke are already seated. From the looks on their faces, both are in full protection mode. Topher laces his fingers through mine under the table as the servers begin bringing the meal to the tables. Whether through the magic of Violet's arrangement or community design, most of the lycan sit at tables closer to Edon, while the vampires sit on the opposite side. Neither group is mingling with the other. Maybe they're in on the ruse?

The meal is eaten, and the items are cleaned without anything dramatic happening. Viktor catches my eye from across the room. He doesn't pull his eyes away from mine as he stares into my soul. I know him well enough to understand he's trying to tell me something. I look at the council members next to us. Most of them have had several glasses of blood and are talking and laughing among themselves. I scan the room, hoping to get a feel for what he wants me to pick up on.

In the back of the room, I see her. Tammy is wearing a wig and a formal gown, but it's Tammy. I pretend to choke, pulling my napkin to my face. "She's here," I whisper. Topher follows my line of sight, landing on my crazy mother. Topher turns his face behind Edon, whispering our discovery to his father who nods to a tall lycanthrope not far from our table.

"Let them take care of her," Topher says, covering his mouth with our joined hands and pretending to kiss mine. I nod, knowingly, picking up my glass of blood and taking a large gulp. Viktor nods, following the group toward Tammy. How did he know she didn't belong?

The crowd in front of us has no idea that there's a deadly hybrid in the room, ready and more than willing to kill them all. Several minutes pass before an explosion of sound comes from the back of the room. Several people closer to the back of the room stand, searching for the source.

"What's that?" Hypatia asks from her table.

Tammy comes into view, holding a lycanthrope in her clutch. She's covered in blood and the man she's holding looks terrified. "Welcome!" she shouts over the roar of the guests. "You're all probably wondering who I am." She pulls a knife out of nowhere, slicing the lycanthrope's throat in front of everyone. Blood splatters on the floor as his body collapses in a heap.

"Silver blade," Topher says, moving to stand.

"Dammit." Edon stands, pointing at two more men who run toward the insanity that is Tammy. She shifts from human to wolf form in the blink of an eye. Her growl fills the room with sound.

"This is getting fun!" Hypatia stands, clapping her hands. "Hats off to the event organizer."

Tammy runs past the men Edon sent, knocking them out with one blow. How the hell is she so strong? She's moving full speed toward us and the council. Every lycanthrope in the room shifts to wolf form as the room erupts in complete destruction. Topher steps in front of me, ever my protector. He and Edon are the only two wolves comparable in size to Tammy. Each one that tries to stop her never even makes it close to her. She's leaving a trail of blood and death in her wake.

"We have to stop her," I yell over the screams of the crowd. "She'll kill everyone."

Tammy keeps moving until she's in front of the head tables. She snarls, throwing spit in all directions around her. "Who is this?" Hypatia asks.

"My mother."

"Kill her," she orders Leonard. He stands, moving toward the snarling beast.

"You are a beautiful thing, but it's time for you to die." He transforms into a creature from nightmares, flying through the air and landing on top of Tammy. She cries out in pain as his teeth sink into her neck. She claws and thrashes under his hold and manages to wrap a claw around the ancient vampire, throwing him to the ground in front of her. Without hesitation, she sinks her teeth into his neck, ripping it from his body with one tug.

"Leonard?" Hypatia asks the now dead vampire.

Tammy makes a sound that is a mixture of tiger and wolf as she moves in front of me. Her eyes tell me what her words can't. The wolf smiles and instead of thrashing a claw toward me, she slices into Edon, catching him off guard.

Every lycan in the building moves toward the hybrid wolf, with her death in mind. Topher doesn't hesitate. He jumps on top of Tammy, and the two giant creatures are nothing more than a supernatural whirl of fur and sound. Topher matches her fight, keeping her away from his injured Alpha. The fight slows down and seems to move in slow motion as Topher yelps, seconds before his limp body is thrown to the ground yards away from the fight. At the sight of Topher's lifeless body and the huge wolf with total destruction on her mind, something takes over my body.

A rumble begins in my stomach and moves quickly through my arms and legs. I double over in pain as every bone in my body breaks at the same time. The scream that leaves my mouth is guttural, and it takes my brain a few minutes to recognize the sound is coming from me.

The world around me stops as the creatures that once were in an uproar, stop to watch whatever is happening. As quickly as the pain comes, it goes, leaving me breathing harder than I ever have. Whatever happened is over, and I feel more alive than ever. One look down and I'm met with nothing but bright red fur. My beautiful green dress is torn to shreds and scattered on the concrete nearby. What the hell? I open my mouth, asking for help, and am met with a growl that rivals the sounds coming from my mother.

Oh, my God. I just shifted into a giant, red wolf.

what just happened?

TAMMY IS on her feet and in front of me within seconds. I don't know if she wants to kill me or hug me. From the look in her eyes, she doesn't know either. I'm like her, a wolf hybrid, but with a splash of vampire thrown in. I represent everything she wants to kill.

I look over to see Edon is back on his feet, but Topher is still unconscious. He's lying in a newly formed pool of blood. Anger fills me as I turn back toward the wolf that is my mother.

"This is quite the show," Hypatia continues to applaud. I snarl at her, throwing hybrid spit in her direction. "Now, that was uncalled for." She wipes the front of her sequin gown.

The hybrid wolf does something I didn't know was possible. She stands erect. The beautiful woman that was once my mother is now nearly eight feet tall. She moves toward me on two legs, swiping her paw at my head. She makes contact at the same time a familiar dark brown wolf jumps on her back. Topher claws at her, shredding the skin and fur underneath him. She yelps in pain and turns, trying to get him off.

Edon jumps and copies Topher's movement, jumping on her front and continuing the assault. She's being ripped apart by two giant wolves, yet she is still on her feet and fighting. How is she stronger than two alpha males?

Edon is the first to be thrown off, as Tammy manages to bite and clamp down on his neck. Blood is pouring everywhere as Edon fights, refusing to let go of the hybrid. The rest of the pack surrounds the fight, ready to jump at Edon's call.

At the smell of blood, several vampires in the building begin changing into strigoi-looking creatures. This has to stop now. This is about to turn into a shit show of unmeasurable proportions.

Topher is still holding onto her back, while his father's chest is nearly clawed away to nothing. Edon's muscular chest is clearly exposed and his grip on the hybrid is weakening. Topher is doing everything he can to keep Tammy from injuring his father more than she already has, but with one final blow, she slices his wolf body wide open, exposing every internal organ and his entire rib cage.

Edon loses his grip on the hybrid and collapses in

front of me. The strongest man I know lies in a pool of blood in front of me while his son is clinging to the back of his destroyer. The pack surrounds their Alpha, protecting him from the dangers that fill the room.

Whatever power that changed me into this creature fills me once again. I refuse to let that bitch do the same to Topher. I rise to two legs and run straight into the fight. I'm as large as Tammy as I slam into her torso, knocking Topher a few feet behind us. Her attention switches to me immediately and flashes a mixture of snarl and smile.

"Join me," a voice snarls through my mind. *"Together, we can rid the world of this filth. We're clearly the superior creatures in the room."*

"Tammy?" I ask as we circle each other.

"I'd prefer Mom, but Tammy will do."

"How are you talking to me?"

A deep laugh echoes through my mind. *"You're my pack. I am your Alpha."*

"Like hell you are. I don't have an alpha. For that matter, I don't have a mother. You don't get to claim that role. You left me, alone, at the age of twelve. The mother, and I mean that title in the broad spectrum, that I once knew is dead. She died the moment she stepped out of my life."

"I'm here now. Let me be the mother you crave. The leader you crave. I love you, Amelia."

Anger fills my core at her words. *"You're crazy. I don't*

want anything to do with you." I lunge, surprising her and knocking her into the ancient brick wall behind her. She's back on her feet in an instant.

"That wasn't very nice," she pants. *"Is that any way to treat the woman who gave you life?"* She charges me and is on top of me in an instant. Red-hot pain shoots down my spine as claws rip into my flesh and teeth sink into my neck. Something red flashes past me, grabbing the hybrid and throwing her to the ground. I barely catch a glimpse of the smaller creature who just attacked an eight-foot hybrid wolf. It's a vampire.

Bright red hair stops and steps in front of me. "I'm sorry, Amelia." *Celeste! No!* She turns, facing the hybrid, and changes into the familiar gargoyle creature I recognize from before.

The two creatures move so fast, that I struggle to understand what's going on. In a flash of red and brown, the creatures are battling each other to the death. Topher is on his feet and at my side, panting. Blood covers his dark brown fur, clumping it together around his ears and head.

"Get Edon out of here!" I scream through my mind, begging him to understand. His eyes squint closed as he seems to understand and disagree with my request. In front of me, the fight rages and Hypatia, who's been uninvolved in the battle, has turned her focus to the misshapen vampire.

In front of me, the hybrid wolf catches the red

streak, throwing her to the ground. *Celeste!* Viktor jumps on Tammy's back, seemingly out of nowhere. His face is nearly unrecognizable as he latches on to the hybrid's throat. Tammy screams in pain as she slashes her claws into his back. He refuses to let go as she slices through his body, nearly ripping him into shreds.

I look around the room at the vampires who stand back, refusing to help. They're standing around, watching, as if this is some sort of show at an amusement park. Why is no one trying to help him?

Several of the creatures that took on strigoi features earlier are still on the floor, licking up the spilled blood, but none have stepped in to try and help. Topher nudges me with his heavy shoulder. His eyes are full of emotion, and I know what he's asking.

Together, we run, flanking either side of the hybrid as Viktor continues his assault from above. His arms are nearly completely detached as well as one of his legs, but he refuses to release Tammy's neck. Celeste joins our attack, and the three of us jump on Tammy at the same time.

She cries out in pain as we pull her to the ground. Topher has stripped her arm down to the bone, while Celeste latches on to the other side of her neck. Between the three of them, they pull her to the ground as I grab a silver knife from a nearby place setting and plunge it into her heart.

The room is silent as Tammy's eyes dilate, and she

shifts back into human form. Where the giant hybrid wolf lay earlier is now replaced by a petite middle-aged brunette psychopath.

Celeste and Viktor release their holds and collapse on the ground beside her. Viktor is injured but will heal. Celeste's terrifying form shifts back to the familiar features of my preschool-sized maker. The young woman who visited me at my loft is replaced by the familiar red curls and rosy cheeks of my pint-sized maker.

What happened? Why is she a child again? I turn back, facing the remaining council. Each of them has the same smirk plastered across their faces. "Well, look who came to your rescue." Hypatia moves closer. "This must be the immortal child I've heard so much about. Aren't you just the cutest little thing?"

Beside me, Topher shifts back into human form. He doesn't seem fazed to be standing in the middle of a room of vampires and lycan, stark naked. Hypatia looks him up and down with an approving grin. "Leave," Topher warns.

"Why would I do that? This city has finally gotten interesting."

Viktor stands, already healing from his injuries, and moves next to Topher. "As you can see, Hypatia, Celeste is in full control of her body and her abilities. She is no danger to humans or exposing us to the world."

"I'll be the judge of that." She steps closer to the brave child, rubbing a long fingernail against her cheek.

To her credit, Celeste doesn't flinch. "When you attacked the creature, you were not a child." She lifts one of Celeste's curls, running it through her fingers. "And now you are. What changed?"

Celeste looks at her father who nods, giving her permission to speak the truth. "The magic that changed me into an adult came with limitations."

"What limitation was that?" Hypatia continues.

Celeste shifts her weight. "The magic only works on the condition I don't kill anyone." She looks at Tammy's lifeless body. "When the hybrid died, so did the magic."

"But you didn't deliver the death blow. I believe that was secured by your offspring."

"Semantics," Celeste whispers. "I was responsible for bringing her down. I helped kill her, therefore, I killed someone, and the magic is reversed."

Dammit, why am I still in wolf form? I shake my head, like I've seen millions of dogs do before, hoping that will help transform me back to human form. Nothing helps. Am I stuck like this? Is this my new look?

Topher leans into me. "Echo these words in your mind. I release the power that compels me to turn."

I do as he suggests, and nothing happens. I repeat the words over and over, hoping one of them will catch. *Dammit, change me back to human form, now.* Apparently, cussing at my inner self works. As quickly as I shifted into wolf form, I shift back into human form. Phillipe appears from nowhere, draping his tuxedo jacket over my naked body.

"Looks like you've caused quite a stir." Hypatia nods in my direction.

"Let Celeste go. She is harmless." My voice sounds shaky, even to me.

"I'm afraid I can't do that. We," she motions to the council members surrounding her, "have a certain reputation to uphold. Do you see this room full of vampires and lycan? What kind of precedence would we set if we allowed her to live? Can you imagine the number of immortal children that could result from letting this one live? No, I'm afraid she must die along with her maker and," she turns to me. "Her offspring."

Topher steps in front of me. "You will not harm Amelia."

"Who said anything about harming her? I'm going to kill her."

"No," Viktor speaks for the first time. "I'm the one responsible for the child's transformation. It was me who kept her hidden all this time. If anyone deserves to die, it's me."

"Father, no," Celeste warns.

"Celeste has done nothing wrong. Let me take her to our island where she will never come in contact with another human. She will not hurt anyone. There she can live her life as long as she chooses."

"Viktor," Hypatia chastises him. "You know as well as I do that the child cannot leave the city. The council cannot appear weak."

"Daddy," Celeste says as he steps in front of her. "Please, don't do this."

"The council won't appear weak. What's wrong with showing pity on a young girl whose life was ripped away from her when I changed her?"

Hypatia laughs. "You didn't change her. Do not mock me, Viktor. I smell who her maker was. It's in her blood still to this day."

"I beg of you. Let her live. You can have my life in return." His voice is no louder than a whisper. He turns, making eye contact with me. "Take care of her." In a flash of movement, he's on top of Hypatia as Celeste runs faster than my vampire eyes can track out of the building, leaving her father in a battle that he will not win.

In a moment torn straight from an action movie, Viktor's lifeless body lands on the concrete floor, separated from his head. Hypatia's mouth is covered in blood as it drips down her chin. "Get the girl!" she screams as she turns on me. "I hope you learned something from that little display. No one is stronger than me."

Topher shifts back into wolf form, ready to fight to the death. No, I can't let this happen. Everyone in this room will die, leaving no one except Hypatia in the center.

"Okay!" I shout over the growls of the wolves. "Just don't hurt anyone else in this room."

"Do you think that you're important enough to

make demands? Just because you managed to change into some freakish hybrid wolf, means nothing to me."

Behind her something moves faster than my eyes can track. A black streak flies into Hypatia's back, slamming something into her body. Hypatia's eyes expand as the realization of what happened hits her. She looks down at the end of the wooden stake that pierced her heart and protrudes from the front.

Her body collapses on the ground, writhing in pain from the contact. Erick stands where she once was. He's breathing hard and works to catch his breath. "I knew if I carried that around long enough, it would come in handy one day." We stare at the creature on the ground as she transforms from a beautiful young girl to an older woman, covered with wrinkles, to nothing more than flecks of dust covering the concrete.

"Is she dead?" I whisper.

"Yes," Erick answers as he spreads the dirt that was once Hypatia around on the concrete. He moves toward me, patting me on the shoulder. "I believe that makes us even, my dear." He straightens his tuxedo jacket before heading back to his table.

I turn, facing the remaining council members. The three men are standing not far behind where their leader just fell. Instead of concern or worry for their well-being, they look bored. Vampires and their lack of empathy is something I will never get used to.

Topher grabs my hand. "I don't know where Edon

is." A group of snarling wolves in the far corner of the warehouse catches my attention.

"There." I point. He's still naked and Phillipe's coat is doing little to cover me as we hurry to the circle. They're turned with their backs to their Alpha, protecting him with their lives.

"Oh, my God," Topher cries over the noise of the wolves. "Dad!" Zeke is holding the giant man in his arms as blood is pouring from his chest. I stay behind Topher, not sure if I should be here.

"Topher," Edon coughs. Blood spurts from his mouth, covering his face even more.

"Tell me what to do, Dad. How can I help you?" Topher's voice is full of pain. He presses his hands against the wounds, trying to stop the blood. It's no use.

Zeke shakes his head, out of sight of Edon. "You can't help me," Edon says. His voice is weak. "It's your turn to be Alpha."

"No. I'm not ready. You're Alpha. You're the strong one, not me."

"Christopher, you are stronger than you know. You are more than ready. I'm so proud of you, son."

Topher wipes a tear from his cheek. "I should've protected you."

"It's not a child's responsibility to protect their parent. You were where you needed to be." Edon's eyes turn to me, looking me in the eyes. He smiles, bringing tears to my eyes.

"Amelia, you are amazing. You are a hybrid vampire-wolf. What I wouldn't give to see what your future holds. You are the glue that will join us together." He coughs and blood spills all over the floor.

"Dad! We need to get you to the hospital."

Edon holds up his hand. "No. My time is over. You are the new Alpha." Edon closes his eyes and stops struggling to breathe.

what now?

THE MOMENT EDON PASSES, the lycan surrounding him erupt in a sound that's a mixture of growl and cry. Each one mourns the loss of their Alpha, yet they mourn as a pack. I step away, giving Topher the time he needs with his father.

Violet moves to my side, handing me a hoodie and a pair of sweatpants that she magically produced from nowhere. "I brought these just in case."

The wolves have begun shifting back into human form, and the fact that there's a group of naked men walking around the warehouse doesn't seem out of the ordinary for my life. I slip on my new clothes and move in front of the council. Each one stares blankly at their empty glasses.

"Miss Lockhart," a young council member greets me. "Please give my regards to the host. The ball was splendid and the drink divine. However, it's time for us to make our leave." He stands and the others join him. "We'll be in touch."

"No," I answer. "We will not be in touch. You will not come back to New Orleans, nor will you do anything to harm any of the guests from tonight."

"I'm afraid the council is still responsible for the matter for which we came." His accent is thick and difficult to understand.

"What matter is that?"

He smiles, showing a mouth full of pure white teeth. "The matter of the immortal child and her offspring."

I turn, motioning to the room behind me. "As you can clearly see, there is no immortal child here. As for the guests in attendance, I'm sure they would clarify that an immortal child was never in the room."

The vampire turns toward his companions. "Did either of you see the immortal child?"

One of the vampires with him yawns deeply, clearly bored with the entire spectacle. "No."

The younger vampire smiles and bows slightly. "Then we will take our leave and mark the issue as resolved. Again, please relay our regards to the host." I watch as the men move quickly through the door and out of our lives. At least for now.

Erick and Phillippe are at my side the moment the council leaves. "What did they say to you?" Phillipe asks.

"I convinced them they're not needed here."

Erick pats me on the shoulder. "Good girl." I hand Phillipe his dinner jacket back and both men leave the warehouse. Violet, Ollie, and I are the only vampires left in the building. Is that what I am? A vampire?

"Seems I didn't miss much excitement in my time away." Ollie wraps his arm around my shoulder as we walk to what's left of Viktor.

Nothing more than dust remains of the once virile vampire. "Should we bury him?" I ask.

"No, vampires don't bury their dead. He's returned from which he came." Violet uses words from another time. "What's going to happen to Celeste?" she asks.

"I don't know. The council has agreed to leave her alone, at least for now."

"Are we not going to talk about the elephant, or should I say the giant wolf, in the room?" Ollie crosses his arms across his chest.

"I don't know what you're talking about."

"Like hell, you don't. You turned into a damn wolf, Amelia. That's not something vampires normally do," he retorts.

I sigh before answering. "My mother is...was a hybrid lycanthrope."

"That's not possible," he adds.

"Apparently it is." I sweep my hands down my body.

"That woman was your mother?"

"Yes. She was born to a lycanthrope mother and a

human father. Most hybrids die. I guess she was special."

"What does that make you?" Violet asks the million-dollar question.

"Even more of a freak than before."

"No." Ollie interrupts. "It makes you the glue that will bring our two communities together."

I look at the lycan who are still mourning the loss of their Alpha. "I'm not sure they're going to be too keen on coming to cookouts anytime soon."

"Edon was a good man," Violet adds. "His son will make an honorable Alpha."

The lycan have wrapped Edon's body inside white tablecloths and are carrying him out of the warehouse. Topher makes eye contact with me as they exit. His eyes saying more than words ever could. I nod, hoping he gets the fact that I understand what he needs to do. I watch them until they disappear into the night.

"What's next?" Ollie asks.

I look at my friends. "I don't know."

"I'll be here when you're ready." Violet wraps her arms around my shoulders. "I'll support you, no matter what the decision is."

"Support me? Phillipe is the elder of the city. He's in charge, not me."

"For now," Ollie answers, wrapping his arm around Violet's shoulder. "You have my support, as well." I watch the two of them exit, leaving me alone in the huge building.

I gather what's left of my dress and leave the warehouse district, heading toward the Quarter. I walk past the nameless, faceless humans who have no idea about the world that is just beyond their reach. The world of mythological creatures that aren't so mythological. As I walk, most people make a wide berth, giving me the entirety of the sidewalk. I don't make eye contact, in fact, I don't acknowledge anything except the concrete beneath my feet.

Viktor, Edon, and Tammy died tonight. Three people who had a huge influence on my life. Tammy, who gave birth to me and raised me the only way a woman who carries a lot of baggage of her own could. Edon, who protected me, even when he didn't have to. And Viktor. I don't even know how to feel about Viktor. Our relationship spanned from pure hatred at the beginning, to admiration, to friendship, to sex, and finally to nothing, yet in the end he was the hero.

I wipe the tears flowing down my cheeks at the insanity that has become my life. I miss innocent Amelia. The one who knew how to survive on her own and couldn't wait to go to college. I stop walking, realizing I'm standing in front of Fran's home.

The door opens before I reach for the bell. "Come in, Amelia," Fran's voice calls from the darkened room. "How are you?" she asks as I find a seat close to the fireplace.

"Do you know what's happened?"

"I told her," a familiar voice says coming down the

stairs. I look up to see my tiny maker. Her bright red curls are in perfect form, and she's dressed like a porcelain doll from times past.

"Celeste." The breath leaves my lungs. "How...are you okay?"

"I'm okay." She moves to my side, sliding on the seat next to me.

"Do you know what happened to...to Viktor?"

She looks down at my words. "He never wanted this life. He's at peace."

"The council has agreed to leave you alone. As far as they're concerned, the matter is closed."

Celeste takes my hand into hers. "Thank you, Amelia. I still have to leave. I can't stay here, where we lived for so long, without him."

"I understand." Sadness sounds through my voice.

"Fran is coming with me. We'll stay in touch." She slides off the chair, grabbing an envelope off the desk. "Inside are the deeds to all of Daddy's properties in the city, along with bank accounts from all around the world."

"I can't take this. You need money."

"Don't worry, I didn't give you everything. Fran and I are set for the rest of our lives and then some. It's all yours. Do with it what you want."

"Celeste. I'm so sorry."

She smiles. "I'm not. I had the chance to experience not being a child. Even though the time was short, it was something I'll never forget. It was the experience of a lifetime."

"I love you, Celeste."

She wraps her tiny arms around my waist. "I love you, too. Stay safe and keep in touch with me. I want to know how things progress with that hot werewolf."

"Celeste..." Fran scolds.

"Oh, whatever. I'm not a baby. I know what happens between the sheets." I wrap my arms around Celeste, not wanting to let go. She pulls away, as a horn honks in front of the house. "We need to go."

I watch the two women leave the house with nothing more than a small suitcase in each of their hands. I wait until the taillights are out of sight before locking the house and continuing my trek toward the loft.

Thankfully, it doesn't take long until I'm in the Quarter and climbing the stairs to the loft. My entire body feels numb. My loft is dark when I enter, and I'm grateful for the quiet. I move straight to the shower. Blood pools at my feet as the water rushes over me. I don't know who it belongs to, maybe a combination of several people. I scrub my skin raw, trying to wash away the memories of the fight. My body was covered in red fur. Now, snow-white skin stares back at me. How is that possible?

I don't know how much time passes before I exit, find a pair of extra fluffy pajamas, and climb inside them. Since changing into a wolf, my stomach hasn't stopped rumbling. That must be why my thirst has been insatiable for the past few weeks. It takes three bottles of blood before my stomach begins to ease.

Sitting on the bed, I look over the papers Celeste gave me. It seems I now own half of New Orleans. I scoff at the irony. I went from living in a city-owned, rent-controlled property to owning more buildings than I can count.

The door to the loft opens as an exhausted lycanthrope enters the room. I drop everything and move at vampire speed in front of him. Without a word, he wraps his arms around me, pulling me close.

"He's gone." His words break my heart. "The strongest man I've ever known is gone." No words will ease his pain. I keep my arms wrapped around him, offering my support through our connection. Topher pulls away after his tears run dry.

"Celeste is gone," I change the subject. "She left with Fran. She left me deeds to half of the buildings in the city along with several bank accounts around the world."

"I'm sorry."

"I'm not. She's safe. The council agreed to leave her alone, and with Fran, she can live how she wants." I lead Topher to the couch and help him take off the filthy jacket he must have stolen from somewhere. "What's next?"

"I'm the alpha. There's no next to it."

"What about with me? You don't have to protect me anymore."

Topher looks up, cupping my cheek into his large palm. "That's up to you."

I lay my hand on top of his. "I don't want you to leave." My words are no louder than a whisper.

"I don't want to leave." Topher gently kisses me as his hands caress my cheeks. "I'm here for as long as you want me, Amelia Lockhart."

I stare at the giant lycanthrope in front of me. "Forever, Christopher St. James. I want you forever."

epilogue

THE CEREMONY

"TELL me again why we're having to go through with this ceremony. You're already Alpha and have been for months now. Why the formalities?" I stare blankly into the full closet, not sure what is appropriate to wear to an Alpha lycan initiation.

Topher sighs from across the loft. "Because it's required for me to be officially recognized as Alpha. Lycan from the surrounding states will be there, too." His hair is still dripping from the shower we shared earlier, and the towel is hanging so low on his hips that I have a hard time focusing. "Eyes up here, vamp." He smiles as he speaks, making it even harder to concentrate.

I'm in front of him before he's realized I've moved. "I'd prefer to keep my eyes on other places."

"If we weren't late, I'd already be inside of you."

I step on my tiptoes, barely reaching his chin. "Being late is fashionable."

Topher turns, pulling the towel tighter over his perfectly formed erection. "God, woman. Do you know how much I want you right now?"

"It's pretty evident." I slide my hand down the length of him before backing away from the man I love. "I relent. You win...for now. Don't think I won't be using that later." Moving back to my closet, I choose a black pantsuit and matching three-inch heels. "Will this work?" I hold the outfit up for his approval.

Topher whistles, making me smile. "That's perfect."

Ten minutes later, we're both dressed and staring into the full-length mirror on the wall. "We look pretty good together," Topher says, pulling my hand into his. "Amelia, there's something you need to know about tonight."

I face him completely. "What?"

Topher shifts from foot to foot. "I have to choose a mate as part of the ceremony."

"What does that mean?"

"It means, I'm expected to choose a mate from the available choices of female lycan."

I cross my arms in front of my chest. "I don't like where this is going. Are you telling me you'll have to choose a lycan to be your mate...tonight?"

"Yes..."

"What the hell, Topher? Were you even going to tell

me this or just be like, surprise, Amelia? This is my mate!" Anger pours from my body.

"Stop. It's not like that." Topher tries to put his hands on my shoulders. I pull out of his reach.

"Then, by all means, explain it to me, *Christopher*."

He moves to the other side of the closet and takes a deep breath. "All un-mated lycan women between the ages of eighteen and twenty-five will be brought to the stage. Normally, a future alpha chooses one of the women to be his mate." He moves closer. "Amelia, you're my mate. You're the one I'm fated to be with. I will choose you. I will always choose you."

"I'm not lycan. I'm a hybrid freak of nature. What if you're not allowed to choose me?"

"Then they can all go fuck themselves." He smiles. "That won't happen. I'm Alpha and as Alpha, I make my own rules when it comes to this." He moves closer, and this time I don't step away. "You're my mate, Amelia Lockhart, and you're anything but a freak of nature. You are beautiful, powerful, mean as hell, and the woman I want to spend the rest of my life with."

"Okay," I whisper, still not convinced about any of this. Thankfully, it doesn't take long to arrive at the Warehouse District. Tourist traffic has slowed down for the past few weeks, making it easier to get where we need to go.

Topher pulls the Mustang to the front of an older metal building where several young lycan are standing.

"Ready?" he asks, handing the keys over to one of the wolflings.

"No," I answer truthfully.

The moment we enter, the noise of the crowd goes silent. Topher waves at the crowd, looking more awkward than I've ever seen. Everyone in the room bows at once in response. As soon as they rise, the music resumes, and the noise crescendos.

"That was weird," I whisper for his ears only.

"Christopher!" a large man moves in front of us, holding his hand toward Topher. "What a pleasure it is to see you again."

"Xavier, thank you for coming. It's a pleasure to see you, as well." Topher has turned into the stoic alpha, putting on his game face for the crowd.

"It's my pleasure. The North Mississippi pack is behind you and will support you in every endeavor should you ever need it." Xavier turns, putting his arm around a much smaller version of himself. "This is my son, Jackson. He's the future Alpha of North Mississippi and will follow in my footsteps much the same way as you have Edon's."

"What's up?" the young wolf says, with a casual wave. "This is kind of lame."

Xavier smiles awkwardly. "He doesn't mean what he says. You know how young people are these days."

"Of course." Topher puts his arm around me protectively. "If you'll excuse us." Xavier steps out of the way, pulling his son, who continues to stare, with him. Something about the kid makes me uncomfortable.

"I'm not a fan of his son."

"Yeah, me neither."

"Topher!" a familiar face says, moving toward us quickly. Zeke shakes his brother's hand, giving him a half hug. "You look good, man."

"Thanks, you, too."

Zeke turns toward me, taking my hand into his and lifting it to his lips. "Amelia, anytime you get tired of this tall sack of shit, I'm here."

"She's not into sloppy seconds," Topher teases as he playfully punches his shoulder.

"Who said anything about sloppy?" Zeke retorts.

"I'll keep that in mind." I return Zeke's playful smile. His energy reminds me of Colby, and I'm grateful for the comfort it brings.

"Ladies and gentlemen, may I have your attention please?" A woman on stage is holding a microphone and staring into the audience. It doesn't take long for them to quiet back down, and she continues. "It's time for the Alpha initiation!" The crowd erupts in cheers and howls. "Christopher, would you please join me on stage?"

Topher kisses our joined hands, before releasing his grip and heading toward the stage.

"What's about to happen?" I ask Zeke.

"He's about to officially be given the honor of Alpha."

"Is this when he's supposed to choose a mate?"

Zeke turns his head quickly toward me. "You know about that?"

"Topher told me."

Zeke nods. "No, that's not until later—after the group has loosened up a little."

I turn my attention back to the stage, not sure what Zeke means by "loosened up."

"Christopher St. James. Do you accept the responsibility of Alpha and promise to withhold the duties of such?" the woman asks as she places something that looks like a crown made from animal fur on his head.

"I do," he answers as the crowd goes wild for the second time.

"Do you promise to hold your place as Alpha above all else?" she continues.

"I do."

"Do you promise to produce a male offspring that will take over the role of Alpha in your absence?" Oh, my God. My heart sinks.

"I do," he answers.

I can't have children. I'm a vampire. Part of Topher's job is producing children. Tears fill my eyes as the reality of the situation comes blaring down on top of me. I slowly back away, stepping away from Zeke and the small crowd around me. I don't know where I'm going, but I can't stay here. He has to choose a mate that can give him children.

Topher raises his hand high in the air, and the

crowd goes silent. His eyes find me in the dark recesses of the room as he speaks. "The mate choosing will occur now."

The woman laughs, taking the microphone away from him. "Okay, ladies. You heard him. Any unmated woman between the ages of eighteen and twenty-five, make your way to the stage." At least fifty lycan make their way to the stage. All the while, Topher keeps his eyes glued to mine.

I've got to get out of here. I stare at the beautiful women lining up, praying he'll make the choice he's required to make and choose one of them. I move even closer to the door as Topher's voice sounds over the microphone. "I choose Amelia Lockhart." I stop moving, turning back toward the stage. The women who cover it are looking around, trying to find the woman he chose. "I choose Amelia," he repeats. "Amelia, please come up here." I shake my head, knowing he's the only one who sees it. "Please, Amelia," he begs. Tears fill my eyes as I turn to leave. Faster than I've ever seen him move, Topher is standing between me and my escape.

"How?" I ask, looking at the stage behind me.

"I'm Alpha. I have the power and strength that comes with the title." He reaches a hand behind my head, wiping a stray tear with his thumb. "I choose you, Amelia. For now, and forever more."

"I can't give you what you need, Topher. I can't have children."

"I don't care," he interrupts.

"But you promised."

"Semantics," he repeats Celeste's words from the fight. "We'll figure it out."

Topher turns toward the now silent crowd. "Ladies and gentlemen, may I present to you my mate, Amelia Lockhart." Howls can be heard from every corner of the room. "See, they love you already," he whispers in my ear. He places a large hand on either cheek. "I am the Alpha who has chosen his mate. I promise to love you for the rest of both of our lives."

"What about a baby alpha?"

"I'm not planning on going anywhere anytime soon. We'll worry about that later." He grabs my hand, pulling me back toward the front and to the stage. As soon as we step on stage, the audience goes silent.

He wraps a long arm around my waist, pulling me closer. "I'd like to formally introduce you to Amelia. I've loved her since the first moment we met, and I want to share this moment with all of you, my pack."

Cheers erupt from the crowd as Topher turns me to face him and lowers to one knee"What are you doing?" He pulls a small black box out of his pocket. "Topher? What are you doing?" I repeat.

He opens the box, revealing a beautiful diamond solitaire. "This belonged to my mother, and I have no doubt she would want you to have it." He pulls the rings from its case, and the lycan begin to chant words I don't understand. "Amelia Lockhart, will you marry me?" Topher says over the noise of the crowd.

I can't stop the tears from falling. "Yes, Christopher St. James, I'll marry you." Topher gently slides the ring onto my finger where it fits perfectly.

**Thank you for reading! Please consider leaving an honest review. Your reviews help me to gain the attention of the ZON, who in return will push my books out to more people.

Amelia and Topher will be back in Ravenwood, the continuation of Celeste's story. READ NOW!

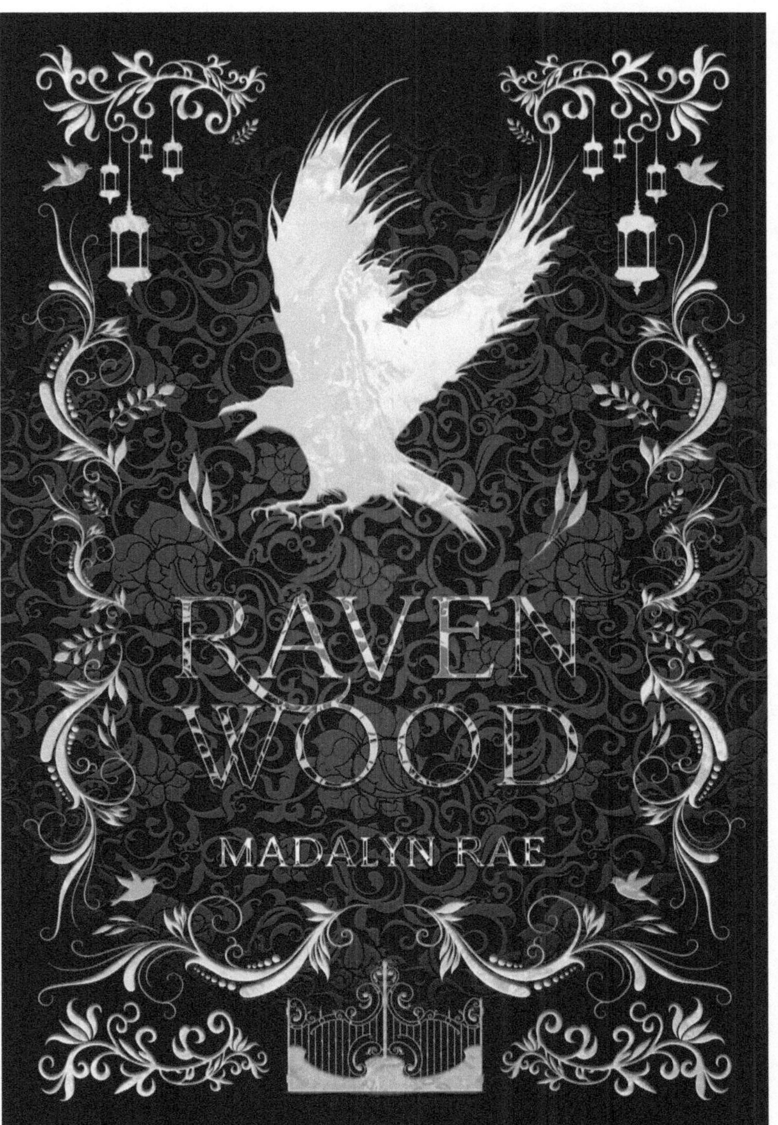
RAVEN
WOOD
MADALYN RAE

Madalyn Rae is the pen name for an author who loves telling a story. As a teacher of tiny humans during the day and author by night, she hopes she's able to draw you into her world of fantasy, make-believe, and love, even for a brief moment.

She lives on the Gulf Coast's beautiful white, sandy beaches, with her husband and two loyal, yet mildly obnoxious dogs, Whiskey and Tippi. She's the mother of two amazing adult children and a brand new son-in-law.

When not teaching or pretending to write, Madalyn is immersed in the world of music. Whether playing an instrument or singing a song, she is privileged to know that music is the true magic of the universe.

Fallen

Lucky

The Elementals Series

Birth of the Phoenix-Adria's Novella-Prequel

Phoenix of the Sea- Elementals Book 1

Guardian of the Sea- Murphy's Novella

Ashes of the Wind-Elementals Book 2

Embers of the Flame-Keegan's Novella

Fire of the Sky-Elementals Book 3

www.ingramcontent.com/pod-product-compliance
Lightning Source LLC
Chambersburg PA
CBHW031143160726
47991CB00004B/1547